Noah's Cave

By

Charles Wiesel

Too much information running through my brain, too much information driving me insane.

~1981, The Police, *Ghost in the Machine*

A special thank you and shout out to Ian Chechet, the leader of the Northern Rocky Mountain Grotto, a regional caving club, who consulted with me along with Carl Froslie, Hans Bodenhammer, and Brian Gindling

Thank to you Aaron Wiesel for Proofreading with such great care

Noah's Cave was written for my terrific sons, Alexander and Aaron Wiesel. They and everyone in their generation deserve a better world than we are handing them.

Table of Contents

Foreword

I've always loved the plot of the second *Back to the Future* movie, where a frightening future that needs to be avoided at all costs keeps the viewer on the edge of their seat. The horrific future requires certain actions be taken in the past to alter the horrific future, creating a bright future instead. The knowledge of a terrible future creates enormous pressure on the main characters to take action to prevent it from happening.

Fortunately, in a movie where science has created a time machine, the characters can go back in time and change the future by taking preventative actions in the past. Unfortunately, we don't have the luxury of a time machine to go back in time. Today, if the world 50 years from now turns out to be horrible, we can't go back and take past actions. Our actions today are the only way to create a brighter future.

In our world today, where there is rapid change due to technology and where there is more dividing us than uniting us, we could not have chosen a more complicated time in world history to join together to ensure a better world for our next generations.

It is my view that we are living at the most critical tipping point in world history to date. I'd even call it hyper-history in its degree of importance, only because technology is creating the most rapid rate of change to the way we live, our habits, and our bodies. Changes due to technology are only coming faster as the pace of innovation is accelerating and amazing new devices are being developed every day. Most of the changes and devices seem to be beneficial and are not outwardly dangerous. Each new product dazzles us more than the last. It's hard to argue the benefits until you take a step back and look at the last 25 years and realize that they have spawned the most rapid changes to the way we live and communicate with each other and are causing physiological changes to our bodies we don't yet fully understand.

We have, for the most part, all gladly followed the pied piper of technology without concern. We notice we are addicted to our handheld devices, yet ignore changes to our habits and our children's habits without altering our use. Today, no one can look us in the eye and tell us if all the changes are good. Like most things in life, there is some good and some bad to technology. I believe we welcome the good with open arms and ignore the bad. Globally, you can say we have developed a strong confirmation bias about the benefits of technology and quickly push the negative to the side as we enjoy the benefits.

That said, the news stories from reputable sources and personal observations all point to growing understanding that technology is changing our habits, communications, and physiology more rapidly than at any point in man's history. Rapid change complicates our understanding of the most important question for any generation; what actions do we take today to ensure the best future for our next generations? This question has never been more complicated. It is a tough question to answer when we don't know what human behavior or the world looks like in 50 years due to the rapid changes to both.

By presenting a potential world history set against a family's history over the next 50 years, *Noah's Cave* strives to give the reader a glimpse of what could happen in the future without immediate, united, coordinated, and positive actions globally. *Noah's Cave* is a glimpse of one possible alternative world based on today's complicated starting point. It is the dark world we need to prevent by taking action today.

Noah's Cave argues that since the late 1800s, the amazing science and technology that we believed was taking us to our apex may be leading to our demise. The great knowledge achieved and all technology derived from it should have taken us to new heights of compassion and humanity. Instead, the science and technology contributed to murderous world wars, atomic bombs, hate, greed, corruption, and the most rapid period of changes to our earth and bodies in world history. The net results of technology are increased chaos, more anxiety, and less communication between people(s), adversely affecting us individually, socially, politically, and internationally.

There are many news stories coming out indicating that technology is changing us and may be harming us. I have been expecting this since starting to question technology as a universal good in early 2008, after observing rapid change coinciding with the first smartphone users. That's when I started formulating my thoughts and plan of writing this book about our future. My goal is not to bash technology. I admit I'm pretty much the average iPhone user who is compelled to look at my iPhone 85 times a day. I feel cut off without it. It fills my down time when lonely, eases communication, and gives me information is milliseconds. My goal is to make you think about the effects of technology, particularly the combination of the smartphone, social media, and apps, for this generation and next generations of children, to ensure the safest use possible.

In the past few years, we have seen remarkable bravery and acts of heroism in natural disasters and at the largest mass shooting in US history in Las Vegas. The emergencies show the humanity that really is present in most every soul that lives. We have seen strangers saving dozens of helpless flood victims. We witnessed a husband who took a bullet protecting his wife beneath him in the Vegas shootings. Many ordinary citizens ran to help those injured with bullets flying by. Why is it that it takes the most horrific acts to show love for our fellow man? If we knew there was a global emergency of greater importance than any before it, I'm certain we could put aside our differences and fight for a better life for ourselves and every next generation. The problem is that most adults don't see technology misuse as a 9-1-1 emergency situation for the next generation and are so addicted themselves that we barely notice the unprecedented changes to the children of this generation.

I believe that the generation born from 1995 to 2017 is experiencing changes to a greater extent than any generation before them, and further changes are coming too fast to understand. Below are articles of interest, news reports, and my personal observations related to my beliefs that we need comprehensive research on the effects of technology on every age group, especially the youngest. These are my observations that led to this book. If you already understand my point, feel free to jump to the story.

- *60 Minutes* ran a segment on brain hacking hosted by Anderson Cooper that indicated that tech companies are programming their products to make us addicted to them and are hacking our brains to sell their products. They argue that the smartphone is a slot machine rewarding people when they go on it. The story indicated that smartphones are keeping users in a constant state of anxiety because of the physiological changes to our bodies.

- An article in *Psychology Today* by Christopher Bergland quoted a new study at the University of Texas–Austin which indicated that the presence of a smartphone on the desk of students taking tests reduces available cognitive capacity of those students versus those with phones locked in the other room.

- An article in the *Atlantic* poses the question "Has the Smartphone Destroyed a Generation?" In the article, author Jean Twenge argues that those born from 1995–2012 are on the verge of a mental health crisis. The article indicates that the more time teens spend looking at their screens, the more likely they are to report symptoms of depression.

- The pace of life has exponentially changed in the last 50 years. The age of digitalization is upon us, and it is more disruptive than The Industrial Revolution and the printing press.

We are changing and need to understand the changes before continuing to run full steam ahead.

- Our young, especially sports stars, walk around with earphones on so they can't hear the outside world and look compulsively at their phones so they don't see the outside world. In fact, the newest virtual reality (VR) technology allows you to wear a virtual reality headset and earphones, engulfing the user with the ability to live life in a virtual world. They can't see or hear anything around them if they are using this combination of devices. The devices shut off our senses and redirect them to alternative worlds. What is so wrong with ourselves and our world that we need alternative worlds? TV shows and movies are full of humans and quasi humans with special powers that don't exist. They take us away from our human condition.

- The average smartphone user looks at their smartphone 85 times a day. It is a dynamic that needs to be understood. I submit for consideration that for many, the smartphone is our mobile portal to an alternative universe where our online selves exist. For the most part, our online alternative world stores and highlights our best features and moments. For many, the online world is a lot better than the real world. Our online selves are the best of what we want to be and show how we want to appear to the world. The real world can't match the virtual one.

- I remember things from the 60s and 70s and believe family life has changed. Families don't talk as much, sit down to meals as much, or do activities together. Today, millennials spend more time with their smartphone than their family, have lost the art of communicating face to face, and think their knowledge of devices makes them smarter than others with greater life experience.

- Kids today are seen and heard, while the elderly are neither seen nor heard, a 180-degree change from the 1960s. Today, children's TV shows have brilliant kids and stupid parents. The way kids talk to their parents on the shows is horrific. Today's parents use iPads and smartphones just to get some peace and quiet, and perhaps because they are afraid of parenting their kids. I respected my parents and when they called, I answered immediately. My kids are great and respectful, but they sometimes don't answer because of the smartphone, even without the headphones. They are consumed with texts, updates, posts, alerts, videos, and a constant stream of information that changes their behavior. They hang out for hours without speaking while obsessively scrolling and writing on their devices. Our trance when looking at smartphones is a selfish place that takes us away from personal communication.

- Everyone is living a life that is measured, tracked, and quantified, both in the real world and the online world. Without judging if it is wrong or right, streets, stores, homes, and nearly every corner of the world are being monitored by camera or satellite. Soon facial recognition will track our some of our movements. To the same effect, every email, text, call, post, use of credit card, or file online is tracked and subject to use by good and bad people alike. No generation has ever had to deal with this high level of observation. We are losing freedom and privacy every day. I suspect that, eventually, every action or movement we make outside our homes will be recorded.

- If you don't think the internet is a dangerous place after 140,000,000 Equifax customers' personal identification records were compromised, Facebook user accounts compromised . . . watch the next ten years as more stories of hacking, stolen identity, cyberterrorism, cyberbullying, and mental issues grow from the use and overuse of the internet; not to mention the health issues caused by being sedentary. People are online right now trying to figure out ways to steal from us, and every minute we spend exposing more information will be one more minute they can abuse that or our information. By no means am I judging the internet or saying it is a bad thing. I am saying the obvious benefits to our lives brought on by the internet are being invaded by criminals who can now steal without coming into your home.

- Driving deaths on US highways went up over 14 percent in 2015-2016 according to a Slate article by Robert Rosenberger with the increase attributed to smartphone use. It's an unprecedented rise. The correlation to the smartphone is the main factor that can explain this. I've heard that texting and driving is equivalent to drinking four beers and driving, and that posting on Instagram and Snapchat while driving is the equivalent of drinking two pitchers of beer. Are we so compulsive that the smartphone and social websites are more important than our lives or the lives of others?

- Barack Obama highlighted the challenges in the age of digitalization in a speech while he was president. He said, "Globalization, combined with technology, combined with social media and constant information, have disrupted people's lives, sometimes in concrete ways, but also psychologically, people are less certain of their national identities or their place in the world. It starts looking different and disorienting." The truth in that assessment is hard to argue.

- In January 2018, international scientists moved the Doomsday clock (maintained since 1947 by the members of the Bulletin of the Atomic Sciences and Security Board) to two minutes to Doomsday. The clock operates as a 60 minute indication of how close the world is to a Doomsday event. What is anyone doing about this? Why this news wasn't the headline on every paper around the world, the subject line of emails and posts, and the trigger for an international committee supported good people in all countries trying to fight to turn the Doomsday clock backwards confounds me.

- Normal face-to-face conversations now get interrupted by texts, emails, and calls, upsetting to the person waiting for the culprit to pay attention to their conversation. It breeds selfishness and insensitivity. Couples on date night don't talk. Daters start with checking each other out on Facebook, followed by texting, followed by talking. What is so scary about talking that the mere suggestion will result in millennials looking at you like you are crazy? The studies indicate a large percentage of texts are lies because it is so easy to lie when the other person can't see your face or hear your voice.

- Social media has made it too easy to publicly state a controversial opinion against another, leading to social media battles. Twitter has also become a new political tool for politicians, athletes, celebrities, and anyone with a large following. People feel pressured to answer attacks and get out of character. Followers push the conflict, too often leading to more conflict. The words we write stay there forever and often come back to bite people in the future. Social media and the internet are increasing the polarization of people instead of bringing them together. This polarization is leading us towards civil unrest.

- If you think the smartphone is not addictive or drug-like, let me come over and take away your teenager's (or anyone's, for that matter) smartphone while telling them they are going a week without it, social media, and apps and see what happens.

- The sounds and vibrations call out to us saying pick me up and use me. This may be a stretch, but replace *smartphone* with any addictive drug (that is allowed to send out sounds and vibrations to use them) and consider the implications. If our brains are being hacked to result in more addictive use by the user, we need to understand the implications and slow the companies that are in a race to change us more rapidly. Everyone must agree that we need to study any technology that could be damaging to our next generations.

- Complicating the age of technology is that we are in the greatest age of hate, greed, and corruption in man's history (one of the main reasons given for the flood in the Bible's book of Noah). With the rich and powerful being so easily willing to break laws to secure wealth and power at the expense of the middle and lower classes, the tables are being set around the world for the end result of almost every example of what happens when a small percentage (1–2%) of people control 80 plus percent of wealth and new earnings. Historically this ends with revolution, something I've always felt was impossible in America—but with every passing day, it seems more possible. When *Time* magazine publishes a cover entitled "The Divided States of America" after Trump's victory, and we have a year and a half of obstruction, sabotage, pursuit of removing a president at all costs, Antifa, and far right hate rallies we are heading to unsteady ground. I'm not promoting this, just expressing my historical concerns throughout mankind's history. In relation to the technology that was supposed to bring us together, it has instead led to the greatest lack of communication between people and political parties in American history.

- With so much information and images coming through the smartphones, how can anyone keep up with it all or know what is real? Fake news and images are everywhere. Slanted news media almost exclusively give one side of the news. Where does one find truth?

Technology has resulted in the loss of truth in media, in our communications between ourselves, and in an honest assessment of whether this is the best we have to offer.

- Tech companies can mandate the study of the human brain to promote addiction to their products, but now won't do work for the government that gave them the freedom to innovate and achieve wealth beyond their wildest dreams. There is something deeply wrong and punishable with both acts in my opinion. These engineers want to tell me what to think, addict me to their products, and think they stand on the high moral ground over anyone who thinks differently. Freedom of thought is not something Google, Microsoft, or Facebook should control. Engineers at the tech companies who study and hack our brains to addict us to their products are pushing us all into a corner and are a major cause of the growing tension in America.

While I certainly hope to be wrong about most of the fictitious predictions in *Noah's Cave*, my study of history, life experience, research, and my observations tell me that we are in the later stages of an age where mankind is regressing, making anything possible. Every generation has an opportunity to study world history, understand where they are in respect to that history, and chart the best future forward to ensure the brightest possible future. I believe world history is indicating the need for immediate intervention to prevent a Doomsday event.

We can't be stuck in a distracted, divided state where our device addiction prevents action. We owe it to our next generations to act today for their benefit tomorrow. We must unite to identify the adverse effects of and advocate the safe use of technology immediately. I suggest we consider spending more time in the real world identifying and solving our complicated national and international problems in a unified manner. We can't be lost in the online world focused selfishly on our virtual selves.

Chapter 1

My Andrea

I'm filled with pain and sorrow as I think about the events leading to Andrea and me deciding to search for a cave in 2018. Andrea was unlike anyone I'd ever met. Striking, smart, determined, stubborn, selfless, and nurturing are the tip of the iceberg in describing Andrea. She was more than I or any man deserved. She was never selfish, like most of the other people of our time. She was so concerned about everyone else and she rarely cared about herself.

Family life was great for us at the start of 2018. Though the long hours devoted to medical school were hard on Andrea, she had decent hours at the hospital and loved pediatric medicine. My landscaping business was doing well and we loved the Bay Area. Our twin boys, Adam and Ethan, were a joyous handful of work that lit up our lives. We had a calm home filled with laughter and joy. The three years after the boys were born were the best of our lives.

My bond with Andrea was unique and way beyond the standard description of finishing each other's sentences and thoughts. We could count on each other to do whatever was necessary, whenever it was necessary. There were a few angry patches, but they were never for more than an hour or two; no oversensitivity, no making mountains out of molehills. Our hearts finished each other's beats, our senses were linked together, and any disagreement of opinion was worked through logically and fairly. It was almost too good, compared to others. She let me watch football on Sundays and she would snuggle and watch Warriors basketball with me (we loved Warriors basketball). I would go shopping with her for hours without complaining and go to all the mushy movies she loved so much.

We had been high school sweethearts, went to college together at UC Berkeley, and settled in Santa Clara. She was the only girl I had ever intimately known and cared about. I told everyone she forced herself on me from the second she saw me, but the truth was that I was smitten from the first second of the first day of high school when I saw her, pursuing her full-time until Thanksgiving vacation 2005, when we had our first date.

I took Andrea to the aquarium and Natural History Museum in Golden Gate Park. I remember getting a bit too bold and putting my arm around her shoulder as we walked by the diverse species of fish, but she immediately grabbed it off her shoulder, perplexing me a bit. Later though, as we kept walking, observing all the different exhibits, she reached for my hand and led me around the museum. We stopped at the seal exhibit, which was packed for feeding time, and stayed a while, mesmerized by the elegance and beauty of the seals as they swam.

After the seal feeding, the room cleared out and we moved up to the glass to watch them. Andrea said she loved the happiness they exhibited. I remember looking at her eyes as both of us innocently and naturally leaned in at the same time for our first kiss. I'll never forget the pure bliss of that kiss. I'll also never forget both of us surprised to be looking at a seal that had swum right up to the glass and seemed to be clapping. We were joined at the hip ever after, and it was the best move of my life.

Andrea was hard working and ambitious. She worked so hard to get into and excel in medical school. She specialized in pediatric medicine and was in her last year of residency at UC Medical Center in San Francisco. Juggling parenthood and medicine was not easy, but you would never see her complain. She wanted to be the best at everything she did. She succeeded in her goal.

The twins were our biggest blessing. They didn't look like each other or have the same natures. Adam was quiet, observant of his surroundings, rugged, protective, and had the memory of an elephant. Ethan was caring, hardworking, inquisitive, detail-oriented, quick thinking and

2

had a positive nature. They would alternate between cooperative blood brothers and hardheaded battlers in the early years, as young brothers tend to do. The times they played with us, without a care in the world, are still etched in my mind as the best times of my life.

Andrea sensed something was wrong when she started coming down with worsening headaches in spring 2018. I kept telling her she was a hypochondriac, but the headaches persisted. She went for tests at UC San Francisco without telling me. When she came home that night, I saw her look defeated for the only time in her life. She told me she had seen her friend Holly, and the tests showed a large brain mass, which tested positive for malignancy.

No one can predict exactly how a person will react to the news that they are going to die young. Andrea had one bad night before transforming into this superhuman being that was going to elegantly and stubbornly fight for her life, her boys, and my future. Andrea was unfazed after getting combination-punched by the confirmed diagnosis. She got the right—you have brain cancer- followed by the left—it is inoperable- followed by the uppercut—you have less than six months to live. Instead of rolling up into a ball and quitting, she brushed herself off and got ready to fight with dignity while securing her family's future and decided to be alive as if she wasn't sick until she wasn't alive. There was no bringing Andrea down.

Andrea's oncologist was Holly Love, a close friend from medical school. Holly was a young star in UCSF's Oncology Department. Holly also had twins, but she had two girls, Grace and Faith, who were a few months younger than our boys. Holly was going through a divorce from her abusive criminal attorney husband, who had almost no clients and was making Holly's life miserable. He must have felt unworthy next to Holly, who was drop dead gorgeous, an all-world mother, and was an elite doctor in one of the most prestigious hospitals in the world. I felt bad for what he was putting Holly through; she was scarred from his abuse and deserved so much better.

At bedtime, Andrea and I spent countless hours talking about life, the state of the world, the likely future path the world was heading on, and what the future should be like for the boys. We both were of the same mind that technology was moving too fast and that chaos was expanding globally, creating a terrible prognosis. We had gone to a double funeral of Andrea's friend's family (mother and daughter) in 2016, where the daughter committed suicide by overdose after cyberbullying by her classmates, and the mom hanged herself after finding her only child dead. We'd been down on the social media-app-smartphone combination since. The online world was pressuring these young minds and bodies to extreme behavior. We felt that this was the new Bermuda Triangle, where the person you were disappears and is never found. We were frustrated that people agreed with our views wholeheartedly, but only accelerated their use and acceptance of the technology.

We questioned whether the American dream was dead, if there was true freedom in America, and if America could unite and solve its major problems to everyone's benefit. Through conversation, we decided that it was more likely that America was not on its last legs if Americans cooperated with each other, but we couldn't be certain. We believed that people were generally good inside, but that they may be too distracted and conflicted to unite for the common good. Below, after much dialogue, were our conclusions about the future.

- Chaos and conflict was growing in government, between political parties, between races, between people in the same countries, in families, and individually.

- The internet had simplified obtaining information but was getting more dangerous every year.

- Our young fully accepted and adopted the technology before we fully knew the effects and potential dangers of such technology. It was exciting and enticing, but is likely disruptive to their development as we know it.

- The smartphone had led to less face-to-face communication. The art of conversation was being lost; our young had more of an online voice than a real voice.

- We were distracted and overloaded by too much stimuli and information by the sounds of the smartphone that reach out and call to the users, much like a one-armed bandit in a gambling casino.

- Knowledge and technology were used to create weapons (nuclear, chemical) that already ended with a war that killed 85,000,000 people, some with the use of two small nuclear bombs. Man used the greatest technological discovery (the splitting of an atom) to make a bomb that could kill millions. The heights of knowledge brought the lows of civilized man in the twentieth century. Similarly, the pushing of new and better technology, if unchecked, onto and into the human body, would cause damage and lead to further lows for man.

- If the path continues, and worse, if man continues to be brought down, then homegrown terrorism, riots, bombs, and revolution can happen in America, just like in other countries around the world.

- Technology was pushing us into a race to extinction, and individuals seemingly were unable and unwilling to stop the momentum.

- We should seriously consider the Doomsday clock time move in 2018 as a warning. At 11:58 p.m., with two minutes to spare, everyone should be taking it seriously.

Andrea and I discussed our conclusions and what to do. I tried to lighten the findings and joked that since I was Noah, we should build an ark to save us from the potential destruction.

Taking my joke seriously, Andrea pointed out that the acid rain, freezing weather, and radiation that would be a result of a Doomsday event, like a global nuclear war, would ruin that plan and not protect us. Andrea was the one who came up with the idea of finding a cave, right after I brought up the ark. I brushed the idea off at first. How could anyone live in a cave for so long? It would take years—and a lot of money. What would life be like? Andrea pressed on with her argument. She mentioned the boys and how we owed it to them to protect them from anything we thought could harm them. As it set in, it slowly started to sound like a potential solution for long-term survival in the unlikely case that the Earth's surface world became uninhabitable.

Andrea would not let up about where technology was taking mankind and about the cave, so she started formulating a plan for us to follow. She wanted me to find a quieter place to raise the boys, away from technology addiction, away from the growing chaos, and for us to live on a piece of land that had a cave that could protect us only if we needed it to. She made me promise to find a new place to move with the boys and ensure their safety. I was numb with all of it—the cancer, the world—but felt it was the right thing to do, given our views on the state of the world. I was filled with fear and felt overwhelmed thinking a future without Andrea. I didn't know how I would see it through to the end without friends or family as support.

Andrea's last months were rough to watch. She got increasingly worse, with radiation and experimental drugs making her lose her hair and distort her body. We tried extreme treatments, turning her last months into the stuff nightmares are made of. She was suffering.

I kept thinking she would break down and cry for herself, but her only tears were for concern for the boys and me. I saw that she was stronger and more focused than me during those months, despite what she was going through. Those months helped give me the initial determination to find the cave she envisioned for us. It is safe to say that without Andrea, the cave would never have been considered.

In April 2018, I started researching caves with the goal of finding a cave that was suitable for long-term survival. My first time searching online resulted in my finding the perfect person to guide me through the process. I can't say the first call with Ian Chechet, the leader of the North Rocky Mountain Grotto (a caving club) went smoothly, as I couldn't tell if he thought I was off my rocker or was being honest with him. Ian was genuinely helpful, very knowledgeable, and extremely patient with me as he listened to my bogus story that I was conducting some long-term survival research and needed to find a cave that would allow such a study.

I'm not sure why I didn't tell Ian the truth. I guess I was embarrassed about telling Ian that my wife and I thought the world was coming to an end. I was not someone who was shifty and dishonest, though, and it bothered me that I automatically felt the survival study story was better than the truth.

Ian told me that a long-term study was not a cool thing to try because the caves are really cold and unpleasant, making surviving very difficult. I pushed back, asking what if it was necessary to learn about the possibility of needing to enter a cave long-term for survival.

The conversation turned into brainstorming as Ian used his wealth of cave knowledge to put together a realistic, though difficult, path to finding a suitable cave. Ian recalled a certain type of cave that he had heard of before, discovered in Wyoming, which had warm natural springs with water pushed upward from underground over 50–60 years, which was the best water you could ever have. He said the warm spring water would solve the cold cave issue and keep the room at 70 degrees or so.

Ian warned me that most of the caves in the area were government-owned. We discussed whether a cave like this could be found on private land and ended with a conversation about how one would go about searching for such a cave. Ian told me there were a lot of old mine properties that could be a good place to search for a cave that fit our needs. Though actively trying to help, Ian thought I was probably looking for something very hard to find. He was kind enough to keep my hopes up.

This call with Ian was the first step on a path that would lead to a discovery. I'm not sure why I felt so good about a 10,000:1 shot; maybe it was because Ian said it was possible and exists in nature, after initially saying it was impossible. Ian gave me hope that we could succeed in finding a cave, and Andrea gave me the determination.

Andrea said that Ian was a guardian angel. She asked me to get back in touch with him and see if we could hire him and some friends to conduct an expedition in search of a suitable cave. So, in our next conversation, I asked Ian if he was willing to lead a team to look for the right cave for us. We discussed needing four experienced cavers. I had already found 14 different properties, some with streams, to look at.

Several days later, Ian called back telling me he had found three other cavers who could join him on one or two three-week expeditions. They were Carl Froslie, Hans Bodenhammer, and Brian Gindling. They could be ready to go in mid-April, and wanted me to come. I explained the situation with Andrea's ongoing fight with cancer, and Ian instantly understood that I couldn't come with them.

I trusted Ian because he seemed to me to live by an honest code and way of life that doesn't exist in the big cities anymore. I came to hold Ian in the highest regard from the first call as a man of his word, without greed or corruption, who was living life with a calm that was enviable.

Andrea and I stayed in touch with Ian throughout the first expedition. I had sent him the following wish list before he and the others left:

1. Drinkable warm spring fresh water source(s)

2. 60-degree-plus temperature

3. Large room(s)

4. Grade for water flow (bathing/cooking/sanitation)

5. Ability to wire to solar or wind power

The first expedition brought zero matches. Extreme doubt instantly entered my mind about the viability of finding anything without years of searching. This was a low time for all of us as we were struggling with seeing Andrea worsening.

Ian told me he could not get everyone's schedule organized until the start of fall. I pushed it to the back of my mind as I wanted to spend these days with Andrea. We set a tentative trip for the start of October 2018.

Andrea's regimen of radiation, chemotherapy, and radical drugs each took a bite out of her physically and mentally. It was horrible to watch a young person like Andrea suffer. For me, it felt that some of me was dying with her every day. Dying sucks, especially when you know you can't stop it. It leaves a void that can never be filled.

We did our best to laugh when we could. Thanks goodness for the innocence of youth. Watching the boys develop at an age where they learn by the minute was the joy in our day. They had no idea Andrea was sick, didn't ask why her hair fell out, why her face and body swelled, why she stayed in bed a lot . . . they only knew it was Mom and they were loved. Time with them made us forget what we were facing.

In June, Andrea told me Holly was coming over to discuss the case and she wanted me to be there. We had tried everything, so I was half-expecting some new, revolutionary idea from Holly. If someone didn't know Holly, they would think she was cold and unapproachable, especially when you factored in her stunning looks. I'm sure they whispered bitch, but she was nothing of the sort. She was a by-product of a chaotic alcoholic bully who himself was the by-product of a lunatic mother. Chaos causes collateral damage that can last generations.

Andrea led the conversation saying that she had been thinking about all the circumstances surrounding all of our lives, kids included, and wanted to ask both of us to do something for her. Andrea, looking me straight in the eyes, said that she wanted Holly and me to be a couple, to move to a rural area with both pairs of twins, find a property with a cave, and hope that mankind doesn't continue on a path of destroying itself. She said we can always move back to the big cities if global chaos goes down.

Andrea covered my lips before I could reply. She said she wanted me to do this for her and the boys. She then spoke at length to Holly and me about how money would not be an issue and it would be a chance to raise the kids away from the rapid changes people are going through. Holly seemed stiff when she agreed, as if she wasn't sure about it. My gut told me Holly's acceptance was more so that she could start over away from the maniac torturing her life. I had no idea if she wanted me as her spouse. Any breathing man would like Holly physically, but it wasn't about that. It was about if Holly and I could follow the script Andrea developed and learn to live in close unity of mind, soul, and body.

Later that night when we were alone, Andrea revealed that she had told Holly everything about the cave and the plan before we met, and Holly was strongly supportive. Holly was willing to walk away from medicine and California and move away from her ex, having already instructed her attorney to secure a deal to pay him $100,000 to move to another state with no visitation. (His mother, Moira, was loaded, but didn't give him or anyone else a penny so he was desperate for money.)

I don't know if I was ever more confused, disoriented, conflicted, and distraught in my life than the days that followed Andrea playing matchmaker. Andrea choreographed the whole thing, and it was absolutely brilliant in terms of a strategic plan. Plans, however, don't account for no suitable cave, Holly and I having to get along for years, guilt at wondering what being with Holly would be like while Andrea was alive and dying, and the drastic change to all of our lives that would be triggered by Andrea's death.

It never ceases to amaze me how you can measure people's human nature by the amount of selflessness they demonstrate. In life and love, Andrea was the epitome of selflessness. It was always about me and her boys. She made me promise we would take her ashes with us into the cave, if we needed to survive there, and that we should spread her ashes after we came out of the cave so she could be part of the newly re-born earth. It was as if she knew what was coming.

Andrea died on September 2, 2018, in our home. I'll never forget how she laid down for a few minutes with each of the boys as they fell asleep before saying she was climbing in bed because she didn't feel right. I climbed into bed with her, held her hand, and softly brushed her hair while we went over everything she could think of regarding our plan. We talked about how to educate the kids, to keep them away from phones and the internet, keep them off social media, and teach them how to survive and be strong. We were all she thought about as her last hours went by.

At midnight, after she slept for a few minutes, Andrea took her last breath. I can remember feeling the pulse in her hand stop its beating, her breathing stopping, and the slow change in temperature as her hand went from warm to cold. I'll never forget lying next to her, frozen by the combination of sadness and knowledge that I had just lost a big part of me when Andrea passed.

Andrea was the polar opposite of most in our generation. Andrea lived to help loved ones and others safely make their way through a complicated world on a daily basis. The way she lived her life could have united millions of people with her example. She demonstrated the importance of living a life more engaged with concern for others without as much concern for herself.

Chapter 2

America and the World: 2016-2018

The years 2016 to 2018 in America, and around the world, were marked by growing chaos, anger, and lack of positive communication between people. The events in the US were becoming a daily soap opera. This was clearly evidenced the 2016 US presidential campaign divided the country, leading to the subsequent battle from the left to sabotage President Trump's agenda at all costs in pursuit of the power and control they desired. If the people elected to govern do nothing but obstruct the processes that our country was founded on, there is no country. There is only divisiveness, corruption, and thirst for power at the expense of the spirit of the freedoms America was founded on. I would even say that the left's behavior (and the right's, when they behaved in the same manner for a democratic regime) should be called treason, with all participants deserving impeachment. The thought of everyone being Americans and talking through differences disappeared more and more every day.

Terrorism, cyberterrorism, division of the very rich and everyone else, greed, hubris, corruption, political sabotage, racism, and ego all were worsening globally. Sadly, due to life-altering changes to our bodies and emotions due to technology addiction, good people missed all the signs that should have told them to unite and take action to resolve national and global issues. The information was coming too fast and it was snowballing on everyone. The seeds of civil disorder were being planted during these years.

The 2016 American presidential election was a long, vicious fight in which technology and social media played a large role in a series of non-stop accusations by both candidates declaring the other unfit to be president. Emails, Twitter , and Russian hacking highlighted the election. The hard battle led to deep rifts between Democrats and Republicans, and new divisions

13

within each party were created. Everyone forgot that above all else, they were Americans in need of one another.

From my seat, there had been no clear choice for the best candidate. My view was that the country was being split apart when it needed to come together. The political party system would never allow Americans to do what they needed to do. I saw no platform that said unite and work together to address entitlements (which were going to bankrupt the country), balance the budget, and provide adequate health care to everyone. The politicians were spending all their time sabotaging the other party and having a political war in Washington instead of making people's lives better the whole time they were there. No wonder George Washington advised against political parties in his farewell address.

During this election, I came to a conclusion that the American system of government was outdated and eventually going to fail. Neither party spoke about the elephant in the room; 60 percent of the annual budget was going to entitlements. Mentioning it would lose the election, so no one said what was needed, namely, that something had to be done.

I was never bound by what was currently in place when thinking rationally about our best possible government for all the people. I concluded that America should be run as a corporation, with all parties represented and an 85 percent voting majority requirement to pass anything. We needed to force all political representatives to work together for all the people. All Americans needed to be represented, protected, and treated equally. The current system left people feeling isolated, left out, and forgotten. I and countless other Americans skipped voting out of disgust with what politics and our government had become.

I fantasized that I was a candidate with the freedom to propose changes to our government to make it better for all Americans. My simplified platform was:

1.   Keep the Judicial Branch, and replace the Executive and Legislative Branches with a board of directors and a chairman.

2.   Require an 85 percent majority vote from the board to pass any law, with no executive orders.

3.   Ten-year terms for board members, 1 to 2 year(s) for chairman, to a maximum of two terms.

4.   Maximum of $500 political donations per individual or corporation.

5.   Five hundred national board members, according to population breakdown of states, and political party breakdown in that state.

6.   Run current national departments as a division of a corporation, answering to board.

7.   Life imprisonment for political or department corruption.

8.   Assign the board to simplify the tax code to 10 to 15 percent of all earnings, with no deductions, to balance our budget and leave us with a slight surplus to reduce our debt.

9.   Review all government expenditures for corruption and waste.

10.   Secure our borders like every other country in the world, except for proven humanitarian causes and needed workers.

I knew I was dreaming and would likely be laughed out of any serious political discussion, but that's ok. I thought through it anyway because the system was broken and someone needed to go outside the box to suggest a change for the benefit of all Americans.

The sabotage of the government by Democrats in 2017 and 2018 was nothing short of treasonous behavior, in my opinion, and a sign that our form of government was simply not working anymore. I understand that many factions understandably didn't like President Trump, but with a series of successes and what looked to be high level FBI fraud trying to damage him, the Democrats began to look like political terrorists rather than representatives sent to Washington to make people's lives better. Doing nothing but sabotaging the government wasted time and money, leading to growing national resentment between Democrats and Republicans

Many living in America thought things were ok. To me, they were the real dreamers. No one wanted to have the hardest discussions to address the biggest national issues. Advances in medical technology led to longer lives with very high hospital costs at the end of life. That meant more entitlement payments for people who need help. The costs were going up and would eventually bankrupt the country. It was a campaign no-no to discuss touching entitlements. I asked myself which politicians are going to risk re-election to save the country and do what is best to ensure all people have coverage programs 50 years into the future. That would be real leadership.

It was clear to anyone who wanted to look at the situation and see that eight years of US non-intervention left a path for Russia to intervene in the Middle East and they were positioning themselves to become a global superpower again. Their early claim of rights to Antarctica was a quiet example of Russia's designs to own the natural resources of that continent. Their cybeterrorist operations, election interference globally, and assassinations were major concerns.

The Middle East's gift to the world was terrorism. Using hopelessness and real-life images glorifying horrific acts (feeding the large volume of video game players engaged in the most violent acts and the small percentage of those who are drawn to violence to feel needed and important), terrorism grew into a global cancer. Terrorism was good business. Hundreds of thousands of people sent money so leaders wouldn't have to work, and the leaders recruited kids to blow themselves up for their cause with promises of sexual bliss in the afterlife. It was clear to me that there was no killing terrorism. The more you attacked it, the more inventive it got. We were always chasing the old terrorist groups while they moved and metathesized into new groups drawing from the discontented millions living with little hope and freedom. It was a complicated problem, especially when everyone refused to speak to the terrorists. I'd like terrorists to list what they want from the world. Who knows; if it was a piece of land in exchange for an end of violence against others and harmony with all peoples, I'd vote yes to solve that problem.

Terrorism was becoming a growing problem throughout Europe, which struggled with the EU laws that allowed free movement and united the economies of many nations. Britain leaving the EU was a precursor to divides in countries in the EU similar to those in America and Britain.

South American countries had many economic issues. Additionally, ISIS terrorists had fled and secretly infiltrated many countries. In Brazil, vast corruption was discovered in Operation Car Wash, compounded with the accused corrupt lawmakers passing emergency laws to prevent judges from being on cases against them and their cronies at the risk of future retribution against the judges. Poverty and corruption were problems in most Central and South American countries. Murder rates were soaring in Mexico. People were fleeing Central America out of fear and loss of freedom. Most in the next generations were hopeless in the accelerated understanding that their future was bleak.

The world was in chaos. The people were in chaos. I've always thought internal chaos is present in varying degrees in every person. Call it part of our DNA. The extent to which chaos is regulated by individuals ranges from person to person and is influenced by outside factors. My belief was that digitalization, as an outside factor, created and fueled exponential internal chaos for the individual. My observations at the time were that the majority of the people in the world were overly chaotic already, or on track for increasing internal chaos. Technology fueled their chaos, like putting a match to a powder keg.

Nature, to some extent, was suffering from the same effects of technological chaos as the humans were. Fracking technology led to increased earthquakes (there were an average of 2 3.0 magnitudes earthquakes in Oklahoma from 1978-2009 and hundreds from 2014-2017 after they began fracking there). The car was a technological feat of genius, but helped ruin our air. Fluorocarbons depleted the ozone layer. Drought was affecting the southwest and southeast, where wildfires were popping up more frequently. I felt the similarities of what was happening to the Earth and what was happening to us were linked by the introduction of altering technologies to both. We were ruining the Earth and our bodies with the technological advances we thought benefited us.

From the 1800s on, mankind had used technology to change and alter the Earth and its atmosphere. The technology mostly altered the Earth in a negative way as seen through global warming and the small nuclear layer marking the earth since 1945. Now the human body was being invaded by technology and it was causing changes to our habits and bodies. One must assume that the same negative effect, like a damaged Earth, was on its way for our bodies. People were slow to wake up, and technology addicts suppressed and greatly outnumbered those opposed to the rapid changes to our bodies.

American politics had slowed to a virtual halt as the Democrats launched a sabotage campaign to disrupt every action in the new government. The verdict was out on what Trump would be as a president. I noticed that the US was signing massive weapons deal after weapons deal with countries around the world. It seemed like the world was preparing for increased violence. An axis of evil was forming with Russia, Iran, and China leading the way, and another axis forming with the EU, US, moderate Arab states, and others. North Korea, Pakistan, Afghanistan, Yemen, Libya, Iraq, Syria, Somalia, Turkey, and Sudan were all brewing problems.

The government became a daily soap opera in the US. From political upheaval, to a fired FBI director, to a war with the press, to North Korean nuclear tests, tax cuts, border walls, kneeling over the National Anthem, health care failures, sex scandals, children dying in detention centers . . . the massive daily flow of information didn't stop. It was must-watch news over your smartphone, with storylines changing every hour, with a lot of the information made up or misstated, and nearly all of it exaggerated. How could anyone focus on what needed to be done with all the useless, biased half-truths and distractions that came at us every day?

The number of stories detailing some of the damaging effects technology is causing to our bodies, especially our youngest generation, accelerated throughout 2018. The findings, such as the Atlantic Article entitled *"Has the Smartphone Destroyed a Generation?"* indicated that drastic change was happening to our habits and bodies, and companies were profiting on our addiction to their products. Our youngest generation at that time, those born from 1995 and on, were not as active, were more prone to depression, and weren't dating as much.

Many of those technology addicts ignored the news stories and looked forward to upgrading their smartphones at their earliest convenience. Most honest people would tell you they knew they were addicted, wondering if the changes were ok. How would someone stop using the smartphone without dropping off the face of the Earth socially? The smartphone was what most everyone was using to stay connected with friends, family, and work. Most were willing to accept the damage to stay plugged in. It became apparent that there was likely no way to slow technological change. It would take millions of people, particularly parents of the next generations, supporting slowing technology and studying its effects on the body to make an impact.

What most didn't realize was that the smartphone kept most of us frozen in inaction, spellbound in a virtual world, unable to stay focused on our tasks. The constant conflicting flow of information and communications coming over the smartphones was hard to keep up with when people had to work, take care of physical needs, and sleep. The major issues of our generation were going unresolved, with no pressure to effect change coming from the average person who spent any free time or energy interacting with their smartphones.

Chapter 3

Mother Nature's Mine

After Andrea died, I didn't care about myself; I didn't shave, exercise, or shower. If the October cave trip wasn't already scheduled, I would have had a hard time picking myself up to gather the strength to follow through on everything Andrea and I had planned. I was not ready for the feelings of loss that remained with me.

I had eaten my stress away for months and started going to the gym once a day to get back into shape in mid-September. Ian had warned me that caving was, for the most part, nothing like I had imagined. He said it was cold, dirty, wet, and gross, but that when you got into a beautiful cavern, there was no better feeling. I was really excited to join the expedition, but worried that I would slow them down and make the search less efficient.

I asked Ian to tell the guys that I was looking for a cave for a long-term living study. I had decided to stick with that story so that Holly and the kids would not have to deal with the locals all knowing that we were the new people preparing for Armageddon. The real and original Noah was ridiculed when he built his Ark, and I didn't want us to go through anything like that.

As far as our families knew, I was going to look for a less complicated life with Holly. My parents gave me enough latitude to move, but deep down probably thought I was reacting to Andrea's death and would probably never move.

Andrea and I each had $5,000,000 life insurance policies, plus our house had gone way up in value with the tech explosion, and we had put some money away. Altogether, we would have about $8,000,000 to buy the land and stock the cave, which seemed like more than enough if we found the right place.

A few days before joining Ian on the trip, I almost quit on the idea. I had doubts about finding anything, was depressed, felt like I would be out of my element, and was feeling lost without Andrea. I asked myself if it was fair to be the only ones who would survive a nuclear war. What if Andrea and I were wrong and everything was going to be ok? Doubt and fear consumed me and made me come close to quitting.

One night, after tossing and turning for hours, I finally fell asleep and had a dream. I was sitting on a bench on the bottom floor of a house that was open on the side and faced the ocean. As I was sitting there, I noticed the room was full of seals. The seals were slowly being swept away by the waves every time they crashed into the house. After a strong wave came, I looked to my left and saw Andrea sitting next to me, talking to me. Andrea told me I needed to see it through and that she was going to be with us. As I told her I loved her and missed her, a strong wave came in and swept her away. I woke up in a cold sweat screaming for Andrea. I remember thinking after the dream that Andrea had pushed her plan before she died, as well as after her death.

There was no stopping me after this dream.

I took off from San Jose through Denver to Cheyenne, Wyoming. The whole time I kept thinking that doubt and fear were my enemies. I needed to finish the mission that Andrea and I agreed to. There is something that is wonderfully simple about starting and finishing a plan. I was going to finish Andrea's plan no matter how easy or hard it was.

Ian, Hans, Carl, and Brian met up with me at The Historic Plains Hotel in Cheyenne. Ian had all the gear I would need to look like a professional caver delivered to my room. I would learn that the gear meant nothing in regards to what makes a great caver. A great caver is someone with the curiosity and drive to find a place or path that no one has ever traveled to or found. I also came to understand how serious the natural integrity of the cave is to the cavers. I didn't understand how my long-term study concerned cavers who felt strongly that a natural cave should not be altered.

Initially, I don't think I could have felt any more out of place. I'm a big-city kid, with that city being nothing like Cheyenne. As we got through introductions in the hotel lobby, I felt the guys were sizing me up. My interpretation of their thoughts was that they were thinking I was some ball and chain that was going to slow down how fast they could search for caves. I was a first-time rookie that could actually endanger them if I made a mistake.

I offered to take everyone out for a steak dinner and some drinks at Outback steakhouse. I was hoping to break the ice, learn things about caving, and plan the trip. We ordered a round of beers and started talking about caving. I came to understand that the common bonds between cavers are curiosity coupled with a desire to be somewhere for the first time. Ian said that cavers were mostly nerds, with some interested in minerals or conservation, others seeking thrill, and a few who were interested in mapping. He bragged he was a nerd with social skills and therefore was anointed as leader of the grotto. Hans was into conservation and mapping. Carl was the thrill-seeker, famous for getting through spots no one else dared try. Brian was a blend of all of them, who kept everyone laughing as the life of the party.

Ian told all the guys again that I was looking for a place to conduct a long-term survival study. I could see Hans get a more serious look on his face as Ian broached the subject. Hans and Carl each asked questions all directed to whether I was sure I could deal with something so intense, and how it would be impossible to preserve the integrity of the cave if it was treated as a home for many people. Brian broke the tense line of questioning by saying there wasn't a cave he goes into that he doesn't think about living in. Hans was on the fence about the whole idea out of concerns of the potential damage to the natural environment of any cave due to living in it. You could tell the idea of damaging the integrity of the cave was a major issue for him, and one he would not let go.

I was very sensitive to Hans's concerns and asked him what we could do to preserve the environment if we found a cave suitable for long-term survival. He said that he could only answer me after we found the cave, since each cave is different and would present different challenges. I promised Hans that I would do everything possible to ensure that any cave critters and natural features were not interfered with. Hans's attitude towards the study changed when he heard this.

With that topic over with, we ordered a second round of beers and ordered dinner. Towards the end of dinner, I told everyone that I had done some more research and found several areas with spring waters near some of the private properties northwest of Thermopolis. Shoshone and Arapaho Indian tribes in the area had long said that there were spring waters with special healing powers in and around the Thermopolis area. The tribes had given the land to the government in a treaty so long as people were allowed to use the springs for free. I asked the guys to switch our search plan and go to the properties northwest of Thermopolis near warm springs first, rather than last. I figured the private properties near known springs were more likely to have hidden caves. It was a much longer drive in the morning, but they guys basically said it was my expedition, and whatever I wanted to do, they were fine with.

By the end of the night and several rounds of drinks, we had formed a bond. I told everyone how much I was looking forward to the trip and promised not to slow them down and be a ball and chain. Brian jumped at the opportunity to officially give me the nickname "Ball and Chain," which stuck with me for the trip.

24

I don't know why Mother Nature's Mine was the property that caught my eye, but I wanted to go there first. Mother Nature's Mine was a deserted uranium mine. Talk about ironic. The property and surrounding area were jaw-droopingly beautiful. You could see why they named it Mother Nature's Mine. This was the Earth in all its beauty and glory. There were streams, lakes, mountains, trees, and critters. It was the most beautiful piece of land I had ever seen.

The property was massive. It had a large home and two smaller homes a few hundred yards inside the boundary fence. No one lived there. There was a lake that was half on the property and half on the outside of the southern boundary. A stream ran down the middle of the property from north to south, feeding the lake.

Once on the property, we decided to split into two groups, with each group starting in one of two tunnel entrances of the mine. We decided that we would meet up in five hours if we didn't meet in the middle.

Ian was right. We were not even caving yet and it was not glamorous. It was cold, muddy, and dark. Caving is dangerous and you need to have people who know what they are doing. I went with Ian and Hans as we went to the upper mine entrance. There were rail tracks going in and out of each entrance, with the tracks joining inside the mine.

We'd followed the tracks for about a quarter of a mile when we started to feel moisture in the air. We passed a few side tracks and tunnels as we went. Several of the tunnels had posted signs saying Danger—Do Not Enter. We could see a ways down some of the adjoining tunnels but the signs, and my presence, probably led to Ian and Hans choosing not to go into these dangerous areas. They probably felt that I would be a liability.

We went another quarter-mile and came across a fairly large room that looked like it served as the operations center of the mine. The tracks met here. It felt a lot dryer in this room than back up the tunnel where I felt the moisture in the air.

When we met up with Carl and Brian in this room, we found out they had nothing of interest to report. They did not feel any moisture and saw only several side tracks. Based on what they said, we decided to all go back the way I had come with Ian and Hans search the side tunnels in the areas where we thought we felt moisture, as that could indicate a water source. We searched each tunnel near the area where we noticed moisture. I was excited by the possibility of finding something, but the others were not of the opinion that we would.

The search of the side tunnels did in fact lead to nothing. As we moved back towards the top entrance, we came across one of the areas marked Danger—Do not Enter. This time, Ian and Carl decided to check it out. They were gone about 10 minutes and reported that they found a vertical shoot that goes straight down where they can't see the floor, and that the end of the tunnel was moist and warm.

My heart raced as we proceeded down the tunnel as a group. Carl was going to rappel down so he could explore the opening. The opening was eight feet across, and there was an old wood beam spanning across the opening. The beam was still strong and could support any of our weights. Ian had already crossed over the beam. Then I crossed the beam, while Brian and Hans stayed on the other side.

I told the guys I wanted to help and got my wish. Carl gave me a look like he didn't need my help, but Ian asked him to just go along with it. Ian and I would tie one side of the rope Carl would use to rappel down around our waists while Hans and Brian did the same thing with the other side to split the weight. I felt pretty good about participating. I joked that Carl was now the ball and chain I had to worry about. This time I was the one getting a laugh from everyone.

We'd lowered Carl about 75 feet when the tension left the ropes. I panicked for a moment; had he fallen? He was ok; he had just reached the bottom. He yelled up that he was going to investigate.

***

Caving takes time and patience. Carl had already been gone for two hours. I kept going back between hoping he'd found something and hoping he was not stuck in a crevice. I wasn't used to the slow pace of caving. It was about 10 degrees warmer than other parts of the tunnels and felt moist, leading me to expect good news. I told myself the longer he was gone, the better the chances were that he would find something. I'm not sure why my hopes were so high; maybe inexperience. I started building up positive expectations based on the moisture in the air. Finally, Carl called up that he was coming up and used the ropes to help him climb back up to us.

As he surfaced, he reported that there were multiple rooms and moisture in the air, but his last words to us as Ian pulled him up were that there was no water source.

I started beating myself up for being so optimistic and naïve. Embarrassed at thinking this was going to be easy and changing the plan to come here first, I took a few steps down the tunnel to hide that I was emotional and tearing up. I felt hopeless and out of my element as I pulled myself together. I couldn't get like this every time we explored an offshoot of a tunnel.

Before I could turn around, the floor beneath me partially gave way. I looked back at Ian, who told me not to move. I can still see the look on his face as the ground under me gave way and I was free-falling. I can only imagine the expression that must have been on mine. I felt a sharp pain in my back as the rope tied around my waist tightened, stopping my fall. Thank heavens I had offered to help lower Carl and was still tied securely!

I was hanging there, suspended 30 feet below the floor, with Ian with Carl struggling to keep me from falling. Ian, who was tied onto the rope with me, was losing ground. He tried to lower the rope from his waist but only succeeded in getting the rope tied around his legs. Carl was struggling to hold the rope, like someone about to lose a tug of war, while screaming for Hans and Brian for help.

I tried to slow my mind down but it was racing. I was hanging on for dear life, upside down, my heart was seemingly beating outside my chest, and my back was killing me. Ian was grasping the dirt at the surface of the new hole I created, like he was trying to escape quicksand, but to no avail.

We were now both in danger. The others were all desperately holding us from free falling. I was literally the ball and chain, and it was not funny. Ian slipped down from the surface as we both dropped at least 10 feet before Carl, Hans, and Brian stabilized things. The rope was still wrapped around Ian's legs and he was upside down above me. After a quick observation, Carl, Hans, and Brian could see that I was only about 20 feet from the bottom, so they decided to lower Ian and me down rather than pull us up.

Once on the ground, I spent several moments alternating between euphoria at surviving, agony from back pain, and regret at almost killing Ian. Ian had some leg and ankle pain but kept assuring me that he was ok. He seemed more concerned about my condition, thinking that I would need emergency medical attention.

I don't know how long we sat there before realizing we were in a massive, domed room that was moist and warm. We took out our flashlights and started looking around. The floor was mostly flat, and the flashlight reflected off of something on the ground on the east side of the room, which was closest to us. I wasn't sure if I was hearing things, but I could perceive the sound of flowing water. Barely able to walk, I raced awkwardly towards the reflection, tripping and falling face-first a few feet away from a warm spring.

Undeterred, I crawled to the edge of a large, warm fresh spring water pool. I emptied my canteen and filled it with the water. It tasted great for warm water. It was exactly as Ian had heard of. It was warm ground spring water pushed from the center of the earth for as much as 60 years. I would come to learn that the water indeed did have powers to cleanse, refresh, and regenerate. The water was warm, but not hot. The spring was about 40 feet by 60 feet and fed down a gentle grade towards the tunnel at the southern end of the room. It was perfect, exactly as Andrea had hoped I'd find.

Chapter 4

Noah's Cave

The room we were in was massive. I'd say it was four hundred feet by four hundred feet. It was dome-shaped, with the western wall being flat and straight and the other walls slightly curved. There were tunnels heading to the north and south of the domed room. I had fallen towards the northeastern ceiling of the room behind a patch of bumpy ground off the main cave floor. The main cave floor was flat and had a slight grade, which created the flow of spring water that had eroded the ground on its way down to the south tunnel.

The others joined us in the room, rappelling down after fastening some ropes for us to go back up to the entry point. As they came to the spring, I thanked each personally for saving my life, but I don't think they heard me. They were in a state of ecstasy. This was what they lived for. This was a once-in-a-lifetime discovery and the look of awe on their faces said so.

We decided that we were going to explore and spend the night in the cave. The group decided to split up again; Hans and Ian were going to explore the northern tunnel while Carl and Brian were going to explore the southern tunnel. I was under orders to stay near the warm spring and do nothing but treat the abrasions I was dealing with. Ian had Advil with him, which we both took. I had wanted to go into the pool to see if it helped my back, but Hans was quick to point out that we needed the pool as a water source and that my going in it would ruin the natural integrity of the drinking water.

My mind started racing within minutes of them leaving. The questions came as a group. Can we live here for 30 to 40 years? What would we need to survive? Would we thrive, or would being so constricted make us insane? What if we were wrong and never needed the cave? What right did we have to be the only survivors of a nuclear war?

I had to stop myself and figured the best place was near the warm springs. The water was about 80 degrees and felt perfect when I dipped my hand in to scoop water for my cuts and abrasions. Whether real or imaginary, there was something purifying about the water. It was water that nurtured and protected life. It was perfect.

Ian and Hans returned first and reported they had walked about three-quarters of a mile up the northern tunnel system. They said the tunnel had a 20% incline going up the hill and that there were three large rooms of note as you headed north. They told me the rooms felt at or below freezing, with the temperature dropping the further north you went.

This report made sense and made me happy. The top of the mountain had snow most of the year, so, without a warm spring to heat up the rooms in the northern tunnel system, it was logical that the rooms would be frozen in the upper northern part of the cave. I actually was wishing for a combination of frozen and warm rooms, thinking it would help with perishable items and growing food.

Brian and Carl came back with a completely opposite report. They had found 4 rooms and 2 more springs. The last spring was hottest; the other, similar to the main room. There was one large room, about one-quarter the size of the main room, with no spring. All the springs met together at the end of the tunnel, forming an underground river. Carl was fairly sure that the underground river met up with the lake on the front part of the property.

The cave's properties were an exact match for our needs. Though some can imagine living in any cave, like Brian did with every cave he entered, long-term survival in this cave would be dramatically easier because of the water sources, temperature, layout, and rooms. It was as if it was custom ordered for us. I felt as though nature had kept this cave a secret for thousands of years and decided to reveal it to us at this time. Suddenly, I felt a sick feeling in the pit of my stomach, realizing I had to buy this property or the discovery would be a waste.

After eating dinner, we drew up a map of the cave. Hans took the lead, consulting with the others. I sat up taking notes on systems and items I could set up with this location and considered bathing, cooking, waste, farming, sleeping arrangements, privacy, airflow, frozen foods, long-term food packages, lighting, entertainment, education, sports and fitness, large fish farm tanks, wind and solar power supply, and other supplies. If a global nuclear war hit, we figured we would need to allow up to 40 years for nature to fully recover. We needed 40 years' worth of supplies.

After he finished the map, Hans and I spoke about preserving the natural integrity of the cave. We discussed laying a thick tarp over all areas we would use, including any cave room where we stored or grew food. Any water we used would flow with plastic tubing or piping that could be removed, rather than digging channels or installing metal pipes. We would grow fruits and vegetables with soil we brought in. We considered aeroponics and hydroponics as well. Hans advised that everything that was brought down needed to be able to be removed after we were done. The conversation went very well. I had great respect for Hans's views, which had a profound influence on how I looked at our temporary environment. I was going to go to any length necessary to make sure the cave was returned to its original state.

After dinner, Carl and Brian decided to go back out to get some more supplies, including a wetsuit and scuba gear. Carl pushed the envelope on any opportunity to go somewhere first. He wanted to see if he could get down to the lake through the underwater spring. He said this could be a one-way exit for us if we ever needed it to escape. We were all asleep when they came back about two hours later.

When I woke up in the morning, I was in great pain. It was 6:00 a.m., but I saw that Carl and Brian were gone again, having left to explore the underwater river. Ian and Hans woke an hour later. Ian had a huge grin on his face. He knew this was a major discovery, though he promised that everyone would keep it a secret. Ian was happy the trip didn't take weeks and that he was right in telling me that caves like this existed in nature.

At the start of the day, I was anxious. I was reminding myself that I don't own the property yet, and none of this would be possible without owning the property. I had received permission to explore the property from the broker, and it had been for sale for a while, but you learn that nothing is yours until it is signed, sealed, and delivered (and even then, it is not certain). Everything is complicated with too many regulations. Knowing my mission, all I could think about was to lock up the property.

Brian came back about two hours after I woke up. He said he was pretty sure Carl got through to the lake. Carl got back two hours after Brian and said it was quite a rush to get through. Carl was bouncing off the walls with excitement at where he had just been. He said he had to take his tank off to get through one spot, but thought it was a relatively easy passage for someone, even someone without great experience. I knew Carl was different, but this proved it. The rush of being somewhere no one else had been is the rush he lived for and had just experienced. Carl had just won the Super Bowl of caving experiences.

The success of the expedition was undeniable. The cave would work if we needed it to work. We decided to sleep there one last night and have ourselves a celebration. Brian had a bunch of beer and I had brought a bottle of scotch to toast any potential find. We had some laughs and toasted finding the cave. Having felt much gratitude to all of the cavers and considering myself an honest man, I decided to be truthful and tell them that my recently deceased wife and I decided that it would be important to look for a cave for our family to survive in, in case man destroyed the surface with nuclear weapons. They laughed when they said they had already figured it out by checking up on me over the internet and seeing I was not a scientist. Before we split up, I thanked everyone, especially Ian, for his advice and putting such a great team together, and promised Hans and the others that I would do everything we discussed to preserve the cave's natural integrity.

Chapter 5

World History: 2018-2032

The years from 2018 to 2032 were a period of increasing chaos and change. Technology continued to invade every aspect of day-to-day life, taking control of the lives of its adopters. You could say technology was the new religion, taking the place of God to those who bought in. Wearable computing usage grew, with new glasses that could access information and facilitate communication taking the lead. The rumors about implanted technology to treat conditions or even enhance brain functions proved true as companies spent billions on human-altering technologies.

The next generation was unlike any before it. They didn't participate in sports or stay fit. They didn't date as much, preferring to stay home or get the latest robotic spouse companion, which was agreeable to all needs and requests at all times. The internet became more dangerous by the year. Every movement outside the home (for some, inside as well) was recorded, making everyone behave as though they were movie stars playing roles. Facial recognition kept track of everyone. This created great anxiety and a loss of freedom. Everything one did was measured, recorded, and analyzed. Most felt as though they were stuck in a box, yet they did nothing to stop the advance.

Politically, America under Trump saw increased job growth in food services, construction, technology, and the energy sectors. There was little middle class job growth besides in the technology sector, and salaries stayed the same or went down nationally after the initial jump and strong economy of 2017–2018. Unemployment was way down, but the internet was closing retail businesses, and the job growth was temporary (infrastructure construction jobs were not long-term). The trade wars that started in 2018 slowed the tremendous growth in the US economy and the cyclical nature of economics led the world into a global financial depression in 2020.

America was open for business, becoming the largest exporter of weaponry, oil, and natural gas on the planet. The world was becoming a well-armed and more dangerous place, with countries concerned about their safety with terrorism and the threat of conflict growing.

The Republican establishment opened up government land for oil and natural gas shale production for the purposes of turning America into an energy exporter. The long-term consequences were frequent earthquakes and water supply issues in the fracking zones. It made financial sense on paper, as the plan was to try to turn the US into a global energy superpower, like the Gulf States, and independent of any foreign oil. The government was going to use that money to help America, risking the negative environmental impact. There were billions or possibly trillions of dollars in the ground in the form of oil and natural gas shale; they had all the right people and connections to monetize the shale in the ground, and the money could potentially reduce the deficit. It certainly was appreciated by the oil barons who profited on the sales.

Socially, America was divided with frequent acts of civil disorder and racial conflict. African-American athletes and entertainers tried to prevent violence in a positive manner and joined together to form a peaceful movement for civil rights and a better life for all Americans after a split from the Democratic Party. The group formed a new political party in 2019 called the All-American Party. Americans of all races joined the All-American Party to fight for better living conditions for all Americans. By including all races in their base, their efforts of unification were supported by many minorities and many white Americans as well. This was the only cause that was able to garner momentum and represent a united national voice for a better

America, as most Americans were too addicted and distracted to fight for better lives and solving problems, or perhaps too filled with hate for minorities to see the humanity necessary to make all our lives better. The extreme left and extreme right fought the All American party and sabotaged their efforts to unify the country.

The All American Party would dissolve in 2021 as radical and peaceful sides of the party clashed, helping lead to the dissolution. The radicals were extremists who were interested in making the party exclusively African American. Looking back, the athlete and celebrity leaders were not able to become full time professional politicians and lost control of their message as extreme and moderate members fought over control of the All-American Party. The goal of a peaceful movement lost momentum. Radical elements eventually split off and engaged in violent racial protest as things worsened in America.

Around the world, terrorism expanded globally, feeding off the hopelessness and unemployment created by technology. Many individuals engaged in terrorist acts as a means of protest. Peaceful protest became rarer and rarer. The period was characterized by a growth of lone, homegrown terrorist killings that were hard to predict and impossible to stop. Who could look into the mind of a terrorist who studies 50 possible locations for the best opportunity to kill the most people?

Organized terrorists were looking for ways to outperform other organizations, leading to the use of biological and chemical weapons. They were searching for nuclear capabilities, according to intelligence agencies. ISIS had metastasized and was growing globally, given the perfect conditions to recruit the hopeless. They were growing strongest in Pakistan and Afghanistan and were active in trying to obtain nuclear weapons for revenge on those who had ripped apart their caliphate in Iraq and Syria.

Cyberterrorism became a problem that cost tens of billions of dollars annually. Terrorism, by its nature, increased internal chaos into the average person by planting fear in people's minds. No one could figure out a way to fight it. Terrorists don't fight like armies. They secretly hide out as individuals or small groups that are hard to detect and fit in with others before their acts take place. Terrorist capabilities to engage in cyberterrorism increased every year from 2016 to 2030. Water facilities, electricity and other public services, banking facilities, and governments were all targets of terrorists. Some even plotted to take out the GPS satellites, ensuring worldwide chaos in one fell swoop.

Russia, China, and Iran formed an axis of evil that funded terrorism against the EU, moderate Arab states, Japan, and the Americas in order to destabilize these countries and create more chaos. A country in chaos is easy to manipulate and overtake.

Greed, corruption, and control by the few over the many continued around the world. People were frozen into inaction from the dazzling effects of technology and the delivery of media designed to confuse them into inaction. Fewer people took a step back to observe where the world was heading. The odds were stacked against the masses in each country. The separation between the wealthy and everyone else grew globally. In each country, the wealthy few used the heavy costs of the legal system to abuse the poor.

Most any history student can tell you what happens in countries where the money and power are held by a small percentage of the population and the middle class gets eliminated. The result is civil unrest and/or revolution. When also factoring in the hate that resulted from polarized political views fueled by social media, civil disorder and chaos became unavoidable.

If people knew where things were heading and didn't have cell phones and social media to distract them, the problems would have been addressed years earlier. The problem was people were too absorbed with their phones to notice that this phenomenon had been happening for decades. It took the US government failing in 2023, and ceding most power to the states, for the masses to wake up. It was too late to fix. The government would stay only to operate energy, defense, immigration, and justice.

America, France, Germany, England, Italy, Pakistan, America, Brazil, Argentina, Columbia, China, Russia, and others were on the verge of civil unrest. The prospect of revolution in many countries was real, and was already beginning.

The rich had gotten richer, while manufacturing jobs never came back after 2018. Companies paid less in taxes and ordered more robots to do the work. There was no trickle down. This was the early stage of the population understanding how bad things had gotten and how bad they would get. People became violent, and even calls for peaceful protests were ignored in favor of hateful, violent acts.

Politicians on the right were attacked at restaurants, with several murders occurring by those who had become so chaotic that they thought they were doing good acts. Political representatives advised constituents to attack members of the other parties as if this was acceptable behavior.

The times were dark and getting darker. Pakistan's growing instability had many worried about its nuclear stockpile. North Korea was rumored to have sold nuclear bombs to Iran prior to starting the peace process with the US and South Korea in 2018, though the intelligence agencies argued it was not true.

Countries were not as open to visitors, as concerns over disease or bad people traveling within their borders stifled movement. It was a world in retreat, where countries were not trading with each other, not cooperating on climate issues, and not exchanging cultural and social ideas.

I remember thinking it was as though we were traveling backwards in time to before the Renaissance.

America was on the verge of the battle it never thought it would fight. Each race or religious group began arming itself and segregated themselves within protected geographic areas in some cities. Anger was forming against the wealthy, state governments, local police, army, and mega corporations. Civil disorder became a way of life. Combined with terrorist attacks, the states were quickly overwhelmed. The American melting pot was separating into its constituent ingredients. You could find the same phenomenon throughout the world. America was always the leader. America was racing, in the lead, towards chaos and revolution. No national peaceful protest worked. People didn't want to cooperate. Cooperation and communication became non-existent. The resulting race wars waged in the biggest cities left people fleeing the cities without knowing where they would go, or stuck in ghettos. It was as though history was reversing itself.

During this period of conflict, from 2026-2032, violent biker clubs rapidly grew in America. Historically, dozens of non-violent gangs existed, though some engaged in crime. Global chaos led to a membership explosion. These violent clubs operated like armed gangs, many made up of ex-military, who would roam rural territories where there were opportunities to profit on anything of value. They operated like organized armies to threaten local populations away from the large cities. They had thrived for decades; however, the circumstances on the ground in America took them to their highest levels of power and profit after the fall of the American government.

The natural world was staging its own revolution. All the computer models of global warming were off in their projections of the speed in which climate change was affecting the world. It was much faster than anticipated, and accelerating every year. Many cities in China had air quality that was bordering on hazardous. By 2026, people were migrating away from areas that were too hot or were near rising global waters created by melting ice in the Polar Regions.

The melting of the ice actually led to other issues besides rising sea levels. In 2027, the melting polar ice cap in Antarctica led to the release of a virus from millions of years ago. It was transmitted to a group of Russian oil workers, who then traveled back to Russia. There, the disease spread and it soon became a global epidemic, despite the reduction of international travel. The virus was known around the world as the "Death Virus" because 8 out of 10 infected people infected died. Globally, more than 700,000,000 people died from the Death Virus. People bought supplies and locked themselves up for weeks in order to avoid contact with carriers. People did not want to be near others.

Chaos was unstoppable. The Doomsday Clock was moved to one minute to Doomsday in 2028. The only question was how soon the Doomsday clock was going to strike midnight.

As I look back, it is hard to say when mankind reached its height and started its descent. Man was going full circle, and would likely need to go underground, back to the caves or nuclear bunkers, to survive and start again. The question of what the exact turning point for man was one we contemplated for many years. Was it the pace of change in personal lifestyle caused by technology? Was it the loss of jobs to machinery? Was it the birth and growth of global terrorism? Was it simply that man was an animal capable of killing his fellow man? Was it the abuse of nature for profit? Was it corruption, hubris, greed, or power? Was it the creation and use of a nuclear weapon? Was it increasing chaos and hate caused by the invasion of our bodies by technology? Was it the combination of all of the above?

The only thing that was certain was that there were more bad acts being done than good, the horrific had become commonplace. Good people justified doing bad things to their fellow man who were not as fortunate, and mankind was losing touch with what it should strive for. To me, mankind's descent was caused by too much knowledge, used irresponsibly, which created too much chaos, too many distractions, and a total lack of cooperative dialogue. The momentum was impossible to stop. Mankind's end was approaching and inevitable, with voices of reason silenced by the overwhelming voices of chaos and anger.

Chapter 6

Hello Wyoming

When we left the Bay Area and moved to Wyoming and our new property in 2019, we could not have felt more out of place during our first few months. It was cold, unfamiliar, and didn't have the luxuries we were used to. We were coming from about as opposite a place and lifestyle in the Bay Area, where there was no snow or mountains and everything was minutes away.

It took us over six months to close the sale of the property. A few weeks after we closed escrow, and we made the payment of the $100,000 to Holly's ex, we were slammed with an emergency restraining order lawsuit by Moira, Holly's ex mother in law, who was trying to prevent our move. Moira went ballistic when she learned about the deal. We had always been nice to Moira, and even allowed her to visit the kids without her son. But the news of our move set Moira off. Moira was not going to let the girls move without a fight. She filed a suit trying to prevent us to move on her and her son's behalf.

Thankfully, the judge immediately threw the case out upon our presentation of the notarized agreement we had signed with Holly's ex confirming the payment and deal terms. The judge ruled Moira had no legal standing. She became furious and cursed the judge to a life in Hell. She then followed us into the elevator and glared at Holly and me. As we exited the elevator and the courthouse, she screamed at us, threatening to make our lives miserable and claiming that this fight wasn't over. She followed us to the car, kicked it, and smacked the window as we were trying to leave. Eventually, the parking guards and a security guard had to subdue her and we drove away. I joked that I could see where her ex got it from. Holly didn't react and stared silently ahead the whole ride home.

It was hard saying goodbye to friends, family, clients, and golfing buddies. Most thought I had gone off the deep end and lost my mind. They joked that they would see me in a month. I feared they were right and I wasn't going to be able to go the distance.

I was having a hard time understanding Holly. Where I knew everything Andrea was thinking before she thought it, I almost always misinterpreted what Holly was thinking. She said she was ready to leave, but I couldn't tell how committed she was. The stoic look and lack of physical relationship made me feel like this was impossible. I worried every day that she would back out. I also wondered if I could stand being with her if she never let her guard down. Self-doubt at the enormity of it all, and my ability to go the distance, rose to an all-time high. Every time I thought about backing out though, I thought about Andrea, the dream, and my promise to her. Andrea's memory drove me forward in the hardest times.

We brought everyone up in September 2019. While it was culture shock for Holly and me, the land and property were a source of joy for the kids. The kids loved the freedom and space of the estate. They explored, played, discovered, and cherished being in nature. Seeing them enjoy themselves was the most critical factor that kept us there during those first few hard months. The kid's adjustment was complete with their first steps on the land.

Holly and I discussed how the adjustment was more on our end than the kid's. We had been infected with the accelerated pace of life and smartphone fetish that had become the lifestyle of mode. It was our adjustment to the property and each other that was the slowest-moving process we were dealing with.

We were pretty much considered the eccentric outcasts of our area, though there were very few people in our vicinity. We were the weird people who immediately put up razor wire fencing, Do Not Enter signs, and had large delivery trucks coming in every week. People just didn't move to northwestern Wyoming from the city without raising eyebrows. In the spirit of old westerns, locals were always suspicious of strangers, especially those who didn't socialize with them. As our dealings with others were kept to a minimum, we didn't really care what anyone thought, so long as no one bothered us.

Keeping a positive attitude, I got to work making improvements to the main house, building a play area for the kids and equipping the cave. Holly was busy with the kids, conferring on all the plans we developed, and continued to practice oncology remotely online and with her smartphone, without the kids seeing.

I developed plans to improve the kitchen, bathrooms, and closets in the main house using a local contractor. Separately, directly behind the house, I built a small warehouse with a driveway so we could accept supply shipments from trucks. I wanted to break down shipments near the house to slowly move them to the cave, and this would be the least suspicious location for suspiciously large shipments.

After the vendors were done, I hired a fence builder to build an 18-foot-high fence out of cement blocks and steel, replacing the razor wire I had put up initially. It shocked me that the vendor never asked me why I wanted to have that kind of fence built, but I soon realized that the price the fence would cost us would made him happy man. The fence followed the land around lake and was about 10 feet away from the edge of the lake. We installed a large steel gate to access the lake as necessary.

The last two contractors I hired were brought in to install six windmills and a series of solar panels. I had the electrician flow the energy created to the house, though I had to run wiring to the cave.

Timing is everything in life, and I think the move to Wyoming was the perfect time for the kids. They didn't have deep friendships, adapted easily, and were not yet subjected to the chaos in the world. They had no idea they were pulled from chaos, didn't know about the internet and social media, didn't know the natural world had been damaged, and had no idea people targeted them because they were Americans.

Kids are the most beautiful beings on the face of the Earth. The innocence and helplessness of newborns, followed by the first signs of personality and natures and development into adolescents is an unbelievable process to witness.

The chaos in the world was interfering in the millennials' development into adolescents. In less than 40 years, kids had gone from being seen and not heard to becoming the most important marketing demographic who believed parents were to be seen and not heard. The parents themselves became too preoccupied with their smartphones and online selves and felt they were doing the right thing by giving 3- to 5-year-olds cell phones and tablets to play with. Electronic devices were the new parenting tools of choice to gain periods of relative quiet. The devices entertained, created long periods of quiet, and allowed the parent to be self-absorbed with their own device, which they couldn't put down.

Holly and I avoided this new age of parenting with our move to Wyoming. Honestly, it was a brutal adjustment for Holly and me while it was Disneyland for the kids. Though they grew up without TV, internet, smartphones, and laptops, you would have thought them the happiest kids you had ever seen.

My landscaping experience came in very handy. I used my skills to expand the play area for the kids on a flat piece of land right next to the house. It was the size of about three football fields long and two football fields wide. Closest to the house we built a play area with everything a kid could want to climb on, slide down, or play with in the sand. Adjacent to the play area, I built a sports court that doubled as a basketball and tennis court. Behind both we built a baseball field that doubled as a golf hole, ending at the base of the mountain. To cap it off, we built a 500-yard zip line from the trees on the mountain all the way down to the sports court, along with a shorter zip line from the baseball field to the sports court.

Watching the kids grow up in a natural setting was a sight to see. A life with swimming in a lake, hiking, fishing, and seeing animals in their natural environment took the place of devices and social media. They talked with each other, rarely had to be corrected, and loved one another unconditionally. They did most everything together and learned more from cooperating with each other than from anything else. They were some of the few, if not the only, American kids in their generation that grew up without technology.

The kid's adjustment to the move was the most important development in getting Holly and me closer to each other. It was probably a year after Andrea died that I didn't feel guilt at the thought of being intimate with Holly. It was Holly, thankfully, who started putting out the signals. I had been misinterpreting her somewhat cold nature, which in reality was her defense system after being hurt by her ex-husband. She started with touching my arms and shoulders anytime we were close, followed by some suggestive language, followed by us opening up and talking one night over a bottle of wine by a campfire. She told me that she envied Andrea and me as a couple, wishing her life had been like ours. She also admitted that she was not sure she could go through with the plan before we left. I asked how she was feeling now and she replied, "Perfect. Like this is my home." Those words and that evening changed our relationship.

I knew Holly had been in an abusive relationship, but the insanity she'd dealt with was mind-boggling. She told me about his affairs, drinking, lies, verbal abuse, physical abuse, and spanking of the girls. I could feel the pain of what she went through. How could any man do that to anyone? She was a top doctor, could have been a model if she chose that as a career, and was subjected to a living hell by an unhappy, insecure bully.

We spoke about Andrea and how she was still so much a part of my essence. I explained how attracted I was to her and how I hesitated to act because it would feel like I was betraying Andrea, even though this was Andrea's idea.

Holly had a knack for saying the right thing at the right time. She told me she had been experiencing mixed feelings since the move, because she was also attracted to me and felt guilty due to her friendship with Andrea. She also explained that seeing how the kids were adjusting and living so naturally made her feel that we needed to move forward and do the same thing. Her words and the look in her eyes told me she had made peace with being a mate as she leaned over and made the first move. From that night forward, relations between us were much closer.

I never understood how tough and determined a woman Holly was in the years before we moved to Wyoming. She is someone who methodically, and unemotionally, does what needs to be done when it needs to be done. If you need to get rid of a scary-looking spider, or battle a raccoon mano a mano, Holly is your girl. She was like no other woman I had ever met in that regard. She was no stand-on-the-couch screamer if a mouse appeared. Andrea would have been on the couch screaming, probably with me next to her. Holly was a stone-cold assassin if she needed to be.

I guess her ability to stay calm and do what needed to be done is what allowed her to be a doctor and tell people what was inside their bodies that could kill them. By no means was she insensitive or unemotional. She was very sensitive to the kid's needs, even the boys.

While we had a great relationship, I never developed the same connection with Holly as I had with Andrea. It wasn't that we were mechanical or distant; both of us were making the best of the world being in chaos and making sure our kids were safely raised in these troubling times. She was more serious than Andrea, though, and I would have to say the bond between us, besides protecting the kids were fewer. We never fought, but it was never love. We worked well together and had no communication issues, but not a day went by where I didn't miss Andrea.

Chapter 7

Preparing the Cave

With everything ready to live year to year on the main property, and with Holly taking

the lead in educating and watching the kids, I turned my focus to preparing the cave and the

systems we would need to survive there for years. The list of conveniences and supplies you

couldn't do without, and needs for sustenance, growth lights, lanterns, medicines, literature,

educational materials, personal care supplies, baby supplies, sleeping arrangements, long-term

dried supplies, meals that lasted 40+ years, fish food . . . seemed endless. But once it became a

list, I set about pricing and ordering each in the large volumes we needed.

My plan was to use the main cave room as our hub for eating, sleeping, and family time. I

was going to set up rooms for growing fruits and vegetables in one of the southern rooms, where

it was warmer. A second room in the southern end would house several large fish ponds to raise

trout and salmon as a fresh food source.

My plans called for one of the southern springs closest to the main room to be used for

bathing, as it had the highest temperature water. We situated the restroom facilities at the end of

the second spring in an area that allowed water to be flowed to, so the waste was immediately

taken away and directed to the underwater river. The natural grade made it easy to flow water

where we needed it for farming, the fish ponds, or waste management.

I installed what I should describe as waterslide tubing to flow water from the main room

and other springs to where we needed it. Holding to my promise, I was very careful that

everything we used to improve our lifestyle in the cave would be able to be removed leaving

little or no permanent effect to the natural environment.

The cold upper rooms would be used for frozen food storage and supply storage. We cooked at the base of the entry from the main room to the southern tunnel, using the water flow from the spring in the main room to wash utensils and plates.

While the thought of me going full Noah and bringing every animal species down into the cave with us entered my mind, I decided not to. My thinking was that 40 days would be worthy of consideration, but there was no way I wanted to smell and scoop elephant and rhino poop for forty years. It made me wonder if any species would make it through mankind's destruction of the natural world.

I discussed keeping animals for food with Holly, but we decided that we didn't want to kill cows or chickens. I remember thinking that Holly would have gladly slit a cow's throat if it was necessary, but in the end, we decided to keep bloodshed to a minimum and only farm and eat the fish.

I started purchasing long-term supplies in 2020, and over three years, I bought most of the items we needed to grow food, live a comfortable life, have decades of pre-packed meals, and be ready if the world headed towards destruction. We needed to restock over the course of time but always remained ready to move into the cave if necessary.

In the main room, the sleeping area was closest to the spring, as it was warmest there. Going west was a family lounging area, followed by a library with tables as an educational area.

On the western wall, we decided to mimic previous cave dwellers and create a painting depicting the full circle civilized man traveled. As I promised not to affect the natural state of the cave, I decided to purchase a massive canvas that would sit on top of the flat western wall. We would use this as an activity and educational experience for the kids to see where man made the mistakes that brought us back to needing caves to survive.

On the southeast side of the room was our activity center, with an exercise mat and the one electronic luxury I decided I couldn't go without; my golf simulator. It allowed you to play matches on any course with the world's greatest golfers. It allowed you to play as yourself or with other players' skills. It was awesome. I rationalized that I needed to do exercise in the cave, but the truth was, I was addicted to golf. I always loved sports, especially golf.

Golf stood out to me as the most challenging sport because you played against Mother Nature and against yourself. On any given day, or during a round, both change as golf tests one's ability to control internal and external chaos. It was the most challenging sport I ever played, and the one sport I felt compelled to make sure survived Armageddon. I figured the beauty of Pebble Beach, St. Andrews, or Augusta National played alongside the greatest golfers ever was the best sports visual for future generations. I didn't really think about how my opposition to technology didn't jive with using this golf simulator that allowed me to enhance my skills. The simulator let me choose to play as myself or as a pro. I always played as Tiger Woods in his prime and it felt really good.

The whole process of equipping the cave and preparing for the worst brought self-doubt and guilt about what we were doing. I mean, most people would think we had likely lost our minds. Wondering if we were right about the direction the world was heading crossed my mind daily. Also crossing my mind daily was the question of why we would have the right to survive when everyone else dies. Couple that with the friends and family, faces and names, superstars and homeless, legends and history that would be forever lost, and you understand where I was mentally while preparing the cave.

From the little I knew, we were known in the area as being isolated, secretive, and eccentric, as we didn't befriend anyone in the local population. We were by no means rude, threatening, or unfriendly; we just kept to ourselves. The frequent truck deliveries certainly caused suspicion. Though we invited family to stay with us in the early years, we were mostly isolated from what was happening in the big cities and globally.

By the time I took a real hard look in the mirror, I remember staring at someone I didn't recognize. I had a beard, was in the early stages of graying, and had a receding hairline. I was still in good shape, but you would have thought of me as a frontiersman.

Not needing to shave daily, get dressed in my company shirt, and not having the constant money game played by vendors and clients to deal with daily was the most liberating experience of my life. I would have been very happy if not for the weight of where the world was heading and the fear that we still could be wrong.

If we were wrong, it would not be easy for us to assimilate back into the world we'd left. The kids would not understand or be part of the social networks, internet, music, financial needs, or methods of communication. They would be out of touch with pop culture and we would be the parents who did it to them.

Through this period, Holly and I ultimately found strength in each other, and, unfortunately, in observing how the world became more chaotic. While we periodically debated our decisions and future, Holly and I decided that until the Doomsday clock started traveling backwards, we would not change our course.

The kids could not have grown up any closer to each other. They had their moments of stress and conflict, as healthy siblings do, but they usually worked things out themselves. For the most part, the four of them did everything together, from learning to playing to eating. They loved to camp out on the field during the mild seasons while Holly and I would watch them from the fire pit.

The kids were so young that they didn't really remember too much before we moved. They grew up thinking how they were living was normal. They knew about Andrea, and the girls' father, but didn't ask about them much.

At night, away from the city lights, we would look up to the sky and see more stars than could be counted in a lifetime. There was a peace and calmness on the land that was indescribable. Sitting there with crickets serenading us was more peaceful than going to a symphony. While the winters were anything but a coastal California winter, we learned to adapt to snow being on the property for most of the year.

You could see the character traits of each child develop over the years. It always amazed me how the twins could have similar features and dissimilar personalities. Grace and Faith were the cutest kids. They both had sandy-blond hair and blue eyes, but had strikingly different personalities.

Grace was her namesake in that she was quiet, polite, kind, soft-spoken, confident, and was comfortable in her own skin. Like Holly, Grace would calmly do what was necessary to do. She was not emotional, maybe a bit stiff, but was sharp as a whip, smart, and handled pressure well because she controlled her emotions. She found herself as the object of most of Faith's disruptive behavior. Faith was the only person who could even start to rile Grace up.

Faith was an emotional roller coaster. While brilliant in certain things, she was ignorant in others. She was artistic and had a heart of gold when she didn't get in her own way. She had what I can only describe as a natural chaos, partly fueled with a selfish streak that was hard to detect but became apparent over time. In stressful situations, Faith would become unpredictable.

The dynamics between the kids seemed normal, but a pattern was developing where Faith always seemed to be at the center of any conflict. Faith was emotional, sought attention, and would cry often, sometimes over things most would consider insignificant. She did not handle stress well and couldn't think under pressure. We found out that she hid under our bed and listened to Holly and me talk. She also hid and listened to Holly on the internet practicing medicine. Faith had a higher than normal natural level of chaos that concerned me.

I hate to simplify it, but the boys were not as complicated. They got along when they weren't competing, but neither was jealous of the other. Neither boy tried to rile the other up. Adam was quieter, and Ethan was the funny one in the group. He had a quick wit that kept the kids—and all of us—laughing.

Holly and I had discussed the kids becoming spouses if we had to survive in the cave for a long period of time. They grew up more as friends than siblings. As they grew, we could see that Adam and Grace were fond of each other. Ethan and Faith were also getting along well.

The girls excelled in their studies much quicker than the boys. It was not that they were smarter than the boys; it was what seemed to be a faster maturity level and focus than the boys. The boys wanted to be outdoors and learn about the land, grow things, play, and fish. Though homeschooled, and with limited internet and no TV, they all grew up happy, normal, and for the most part, calm. We felt that having no technology in their lives would lead to less chaos and conflict as they grew up.

With all the preparations of the land and cave, and the growing global chaos, it would have been easy to lose sight of how precious a period of time the development of the kids represented. Before you blink, they are asking harder questions, accelerating their knowledge base, learning how to cooperate, learning about their internal natures, and becoming teenagers. We raised them to go without online personas or social networks. They were off the grid, and we felt their lives would be better that way. To those living on the grid, we were keeping them in a bubble.

Moira, as promised, continued pestering us. Moira was the kind of lady who would tell anyone the most obnoxious thing that could be said, as if a list of the most obnoxious things that could be said was present and she had the innate ability to pick and say the worst thing on the list. She was an unhappy, large woman, who had buried her husband early. We joked that he was probably looking for a way to die rather than have to listen to Moira. We thought the payment to Holly's ex meant we would never have to deal with their family again. We were grossly unprepared for Moira, though. Her mouth and methods would become a major issue for us over time.

Moira was in contact with Holly from 2019 on, trying to get her to bring the kids to the Bay Area for a visit. Holly was nice in gently refusing and letting her know that we had come to an agreement with her son and were not obligated to her as a grandmother. After a while, Moira decided she was going to come to Wyoming to see the kids. Holly and I discussed it and told her it was ok to come for a few-hour visit with us over dinner, trying to avoid a larger conflict. It was a mistake we would regret.

Moira, more than anything, was an unhappy, chaotic person who ruined everything she touched. She was nosy, judgmental, critical, and obnoxious during the visit. The girls were somewhat afraid of her; they had not seen her in a while and were scared by her loud nature. Holly and I made our biggest mistake ever when we allowed the girls to walk Moira around the property. That's when Faith told Moira about our secret cave (we found out that Faith had overheard Holly and me talking about the cave when she used to hide under our bed and listen to us without us knowing). Moira came barging in, demanding we show her the cave. We refused to show her the cave and brushed it off as if it was nothing when Moira asked us about it.

When we said goodbye, Moira told us that we were crazy for isolating the girls and not living a normal life. She informed us that she was going to pursue custody, even if she had to move to Wyoming to do it. Moira had money, loved conflict, and was bored, which made for a horrible mixture of problems for us.

Within weeks after she left, we were served with a series of lawsuits, the first of which by Moira, and bombarded with stories in the local press. We even had child services schedule a visit to check on the kids and make sure they were safe and healthy. They demanded access to the cave. With these steps, word about the cave got out. The kids passed the child services visit with flying colors, the cave was deemed safe, but our preparations and lifestyle, which we'd fought so hard to keep private, was now a trending story.

The net result was that the cave was no longer a secret and we were branded as crazy people in the local papers, who never even asked to interview us. I was branded as the Delusional Noah who, with Holly, shut our kids out from the rest of the world by not allowing them to engage in online lifestyles, and believed the world was coming to an end in the near future. After these events I knew how the biblical Noah felt.

Moira didn't stop with her lawsuit. She organized some locals to join her in a protest at the entrance to the property. Moira, megaphone in hand, peppered us with insults and calls for Grace and Faith. Local residents responded positively to Moira's efforts.

The timing of this assault on our peace and quiet, and our rights as parents to do what we felt was best for our kids, was more than a nuisance. This was a rich lady using power instead of law to interfere in our lives and decisions. We were not a cult; we were raising educated, caring kids who were living a simpler lifestyle in a world getting more chaotic by the day.

We had always debated with ourselves whether what we were doing was extreme, but we always came to the conclusion that there was no measure for extreme if we were right. I could argue that keeping your face buried in front of a cell phone all day with speakers blasting music in your ears, effectively shutting you out from typical human interactions, is more extreme than the choices we'd made for our kids.

Why is it that anyone not following the path taken by most everyone else is so easily identified as strange, or weird, and should thereby be subjected to group interference in their life as punishment? Protesters came by the dozens as the story went viral.

As a direct result of Moira's interference, I spent the next two years fighting a series of lawsuits in Pro Per. The first one filed by Moira for custody of the girls was thrown out quickly by the judge, who was getting frustrated with Moira, as she kept interrupting her lawyer and the judge and she told both of them they were small-town idiots. The judge was smart, though, and had been indicating all along that no law exists for a grandmother to get custody or visitation. We were extremely lucky the kids did not have to testify. The courtroom burst into a chorus of boos at the judge's decision. The public had already decided Holly and I were wrong and should be punished for the lifestyle we chose for our family.

The next case was by the state, who wanted to regulate the water from the springs in the caves as part of ensuring the downstream supply would not get shut off or completely diverted. This case scared me because I was worried that a state-appointed judge would side with the state. But, I studied other cases, and the law, and argued my tail off that there was no precedence for such a law because it was groundwater. I also offered a signed agreement that no such water diversion would be taken on our part. Again, the judge followed the law and ruled in our favor as a hateful courtroom jeered the decision.

The final case was from the US government, who pursued the property in an eminent domain suit. The suit was under the claim of uranium mining, but I saw through this, as the government had refused buying the property for decades for such purpose. I actually think they wanted to own the cave as an asset. There was no doubt the cave was a unique property. I knew I was going to lose this case unless a miracle happened. That miracle happened when the federal government shut down before the court date. It was a bitter-sweet victory.

These cases gave us publicity we never wanted and attention we tried to avoid at all costs. We were ostracized for keeping our kids away from technology and pop culture. Our kids were hardworking, educated, and courteous, but we for sure did not fit into the box most people lived in. I had never been looked at as an oddball, but Moira made sure that the oddball picture of Holly and me was the only one anyone painted of us. We stayed silent, with our heads looking straight at our target with laser focus through it all.

While Moira failed in her legal efforts, she succeeded in taking away our privacy. Suspicions and fears about our 18-foot-high walls and secret cave ran amok. When Holly and I went to town from time to time, it was clear we were outsiders to be scorned. It was even hard to get friendly vendors, no matter how much money we spent. In many ways, we were the ultimate outcasts because we chose to isolate ourselves and our kids from the locals and the growing chaos in the world.

We had never planned to make security a major undertaking, but when the federal government fell and the states took power, we started to worry about defense. I worried about what would happen if the state decided to try to seize the property or if the state itself fell and armed people tried to access our property. What would we do if chaos reigned and there was no law, police, or troops to protect our freedom?

We were against guns, and killing, but we were more against dying as targets of others who were armed. We were now targets because of the notoriety, and common sense dictated that we needed to protect ourselves from the growing turmoil in the world. For the coming years, I bought weapons and studied how to build land mines and set booby traps. With growing chaos came growing concern about protection, especially with the revolutionary activities growing in North America and globally.

***

We had decided that when all the kids were 13, we would tell them everything about the cave. When that time came, we told them why we looked for a property with a cave, why we moved to live a quiet and isolated life, and that we did it in case the world became uninhabitable. The kids took the news well except for Faith, who was unusually silent for several days before breaking out in tears daily for several months. Faith was genuinely positive and felt like we had given up hope. It took all of us to collectively tell her that we only built out the cave *in case* there was no hope left in the world. We explained that we needed to maintain hope and faith in one another and maintain civilized man's ideals. I credit Grace and the boys with getting Faith over her fears. No one could blame her. Anyone digesting that your mom and stepdad feel that the world is coming to an end could have reacted like Faith.

From this age on, the kids took on great responsibility in helping prepare the cave and farming in the cave. We used wind and solar power to feed growth lights and we grew a fantastic assortment of fruits and vegetables. Holly and the girls took over all the growing activities, organizing all the inventory of supplies we'd ordered. Holly was amazing in arranging everything we would need to live as comfortably as we could.

One of the main challenges we faced was drilling a hole from the surface to one of the southern rooms for us to place a periscope. We wanted to monitor what was happening on the surface to know when we could safely emerge from the cave. We also wanted to observe if anything dangerous was on the property. My only concern from a safety point of view was an approach from the south, but regardless, we found a place that provided a 360-degree view.

Another challenge was how we would seal ourselves in the cave when the time came that we needed to enter the cave for a long period of time. We contemplated cement walls and large steel doors, but finally decided we would use both a 2-inch steel door and use explosives to block access to the cave when we entered to make it nearly impossible to exit or enter the cave. Our only way out would be the underground water passage that led to the lake or digging out the tunnel we exploded to block the cave access while opening the steel door from the inside. We believed that the passage would be our best bet, so we purchased dozens of oxygen tanks and scuba gear and learned how to use and maintain them.

Our plan to enter the cave if the time came was for the boys to lead the group, followed by Holly and the girls, followed by me. I would come in last after setting booby traps in the cave tunnel to protect against intruders. After I arrived to the entrance of the cave, we would blow the passage leading to the cave and shut the steel door. We practiced the entrance plan several times per year to ready ourselves in case the time came.

***

Time started going by faster and faster each year that went by. Someone had once told me that life was like a roll of toilet paper in that every time around the roll is one year. At the start, a year around the roll seems to take a long time. After each year, time goes by even faster. Towards the end, a year it goes by at light-speed. I started believing this metaphor for the first time during these years of my life as we finished preparing the cave.

It was hard to transport supplies in the winter months, so we used those months to organize the cave and to test living in the cave for days or weeks at a time. These days would prove themselves to be very valuable in getting us all accustomed to living in the cave. We were happy and at peace when we were all together. It didn't seem unnatural at all. It seemed like a protective and nurturing environment for all of us.

It was easy living in the cave when we were free to come and go as we wanted. I worried about having to enter with no option of exiting. Spending a few weeks in the cave felt like a family vacation. What would happen when we had to enter without the option of leaving was anyone's guess.

In 2030, our biggest challenge arrived with the arrival of a biker gang into northwest Wyoming. One day, I heard someone honking at the front gate on a motorcycle. I ignored him for a while, but then I started walking over. The person was on a Harley Davidson motorcycle and was asking about directions. He seemed to be unthreatening from a distance. I stayed about 40 feet away as he asked me how to get to Thermopolis. The guy was built like a football player, wore dark sunglasses, and had a heavy black beard. As I was giving him directions, I noticed he had what I can only describe as a caveman's club affixed onto the back of his motorcycle. I was a bit concerned that this wasn't about getting directions, but I helped anyway, concerned about what his intentions were.

While giving him directions when Holly came outside and walked down the driveway to see what was happening. Looking back I saw Holly in a long, white dress, which was see-through with the sun behind her. She was quite a sight to see, but was not a sight I wanted to share with a stranger who now looked like he was in a trance. He scooted off with a loud rev of his motorcycle. As he left, I saw that he had a gang emblem on the back of his jacket. The patch depicted Satan kicking a person in the rear, as if giving him the boot out of Hell.

The next day, the same biker and at least twenty others set up camp outside our front gate. Our new visitors were from the Hell's Rejects Biker Club. We were now a target. I was so thankful that we'd built the fence, I purchased weapons, and I studied about land mines and booby traps, but I was fearful of what they would do if they wanted to inhabit our property and cave. Violent biker gangs were usually made up of mercenaries who preferred living life with total freedom and ability to rain terror. They most certainly heard about our property and the cave from the locals.

The club members came and went for days, presenting no threat besides sitting outside our property on the other side of the road. I was not concerned with perimeter defense because we had enough land mines to cause major damage to any breaches of the perimeter fence onto the property. The kids knew they were not allowed near the fences and we decided to stay out of sight.

The mere presence of the club was intimidating and gave us a taste of what was happening in the cities and states around America and the world. Personal safety guaranteed by the government was no longer a given. Mankind was becoming less civil and more violent, affecting the day-to-day life of all Americans. This was not the America our founders envisioned.

We debated whether we should just go shut ourselves in the cave, but decided that without a Doomsday event, we would not enter the cave. The kids and Holly were outwardly panicked. Faith was hysterical. Grace was concerned. Everyone was scared at the physical threat. We all took shifts watching the front gate. I don't remember ever having this level of fear in my life. Seeing the kids so scared was new and my stress grew to new heights. I don't know how I remained outwardly calm. Inside I was a mess who was worried about an all-out assault.

The boys and girls had gone through gun training with Holly and me and were more than capable of shooting accurately if it came down to it. It was the last thing we wanted to think about or prepare for, but mankind was regressing and defense was a necessary skill for all of us to master. The boys and Grace slowly began to calm down and realize the magnitude of the situation and what we needed to prepare for. Faith continued to be an emotional wreck. Holly was quiet and had a blank stare, as if reliving a bad memory.

After three stressful days, I left a note on the outside of the gate early one morning saying: "Please go. I will give you a demonstration why at 10:00 a.m." I saw that they'd received the note at about 7:00 a.m. At ten, with the bikers looking on, I released a rope that dropped a sandbag on a land mine close to the gate causing a huge explosion and delivering my message.

The bikers didn't know we had planted mines on the whole property boundary near the fencing several years ago. That previous night, I had planted dozens more mines on the dirt driveway and around the lake. In hindsight, I probably should not have tried to play their game, but we wanted to try to scare them away from us. We were not built for violence and were against killing another human.

Later that night, a land mine was set off on Holly's watch. The noise rattled everyone. I grabbed my rifle and handgun and rushed down to the den with the kids following me to see if anyone breached the property. Holly, the kids, and I looked through the window and saw that it was a mine on the road near the front gate. We didn't see anyone on the property, though it was fairly dark. Two minutes later, a second mine one went off near the lake. We were all paralyzed with fear. Faith was sobbing uncontrollably. If they all attacked en masse, we were going to die. These were professionals and we stood almost no chance despite the mines and our weapons.

We knelt by the windows in the den, frozen in fear, for hours. The boys and girls were next to us, ready to fight if necessary, but nothing happened. At dawn, we heard the rev of the bikes as the gang left. A few hours later, I went out to see what had happened.

After investigating, I saw that they were only testing the area for mines to see if I was bluffing or not. They had thrown dozens of heavy steel balls (most likely from the steel and ball bearing plants down the interstate) over the fence, searching for a way to get onto the property. The mines going off dissuaded them. Thank goodness there were no bodies; I don't know if the kids or I could bear seeing that.

As I walked towards the gate, I saw a piece of paper on the fence. I walked over carefully, suspecting a trap, and slowly grabbed the note the bikers had left. It read: "We'll be back. Say hi to your wife!"

Chapter 8

Doomsday: 9/18/2032

By 2032, you could feel the momentum of unrest, despair, and aggression grow to unparalleled heights globally. The event that accelerated the path to Doomsday was the seizure of the Pakistani nuclear arsenal by ISIS terrorists during the revolution in Pakistan, which started in 2030 and toppled Pakistani government control.

On 9/11/2032, ISIS gave the nations of the world notice that it had placed 25 nuclear weapons around the world in New York, Los Angeles, Chicago, Dallas, Mexico City, Hong Kong, Shanghai, Berlin, Paris, Madrid, Moscow, St. Petersburg, Buenos Aires, Tokyo, Sao Paulo, Seoul, Mumbai, Jakarta, Lagos, London, Rome, Toronto, Bangkok, Johannesburg, and Santiago. They threatened to explode a device in one of the cities if their demands were not met in one week. Their key demands were for $500,000,000,000 dollars and for all of Iraq as a caliphate, including economic guarantees for purchasing oil from their caliphate.

The world community was split on what to do. What remained of the global intelligence community had decided it was a bluff and impossible for ISIS to have placed the bombs in these cities. They knew ISIS indeed did control the arsenal, but they were certain they could not have executed such a plan. The old policy of you don't negotiate with terrorists was deployed.

The masses of the world pleaded for the leaders to pay them. Many governments, sided with the masses, and the debate continued as the last hours approached.

Not to be left out of the party, and not wanting to miss an opportunity, Iran launched a preemptive nuclear attack on Israel, using the missiles they had purchased from North Korea, which failed when the Israeli missile defense systems intercepted and destroyed the nuclear warheads. Israel, in defense of itself, struck Iran with a massive non-nuclear missile attack leveling every major city. Iran, trying to destroy Israel, was itself destroyed.

ISIS then went into action and exploded nuclear devices in Moscow, New York, and London, as a demonstration of their intentions. All hell was breaking loose. The final act that accelerated Doomsday was Russia deciding they would take the opportunity to strike the US. They launched a preemptive attack of one hundred and sixty 100-kiloton nuclear warheads at the US. Some of the warheads were EMPs (Electromagnetic Pulse) devices that knocked out a significant portion of the American electric grid, shutting off the water, oil, and gas supply systems. While some of the warheads were destroyed, others were not.

The US retaliated. The American response was swift and vicious, with nuclear warheads delivered from submarines and silos aimed at China and Russia. This triggered a massive response from the Chinese against the US. By the time ISIS blew up their remaining bombs, nuclear bomb technology had stopped man's rule of the earth, poisoned the world's surface and atmosphere, and made man an endangered and almost extinct species.

There would be no announcement of the Doomsday clock striking midnight. Holly was monitoring the internet for news but unable to ascertain the truth. When power went out after the Russians EMPs, we decided to make our move to the cave. We had practiced the move in case we had to leave in a rush, and executed that plan. As we left the house, we could see and hear that the Hell's Rejects had returned, along with dozens of trucks and people who were near the front gate of the property trying to break down the security fence and gain access. They wanted to force themselves into our cave.

A hundred yards from the house, Ethan told me he had to run back to get his lizard. We argued, but I let him go, since I thought the fence would not be easily broken and it would only take a minute. We decided to switch positions; Ethan was supposed to take the lead with Adam, and I was to go last and set the final booby traps to prevent others from entering the tunnel system. Instead, I ran into the lead. I looked back, confirming that Ethan was on his way back. I was proud that he cared so much about life to save his pet lizard. Boy was I dumb. The second he left the house, a massive explosion blew open the front gate to the property.

As Ethan raced up the mountain trying to catch up with us, the bikers and some locals entered the property. Some were on bikes, others in trucks. Now, we were all in a race for our lives. Total chaos ensued as a dozen or more land mines went off near the property entrance. The bikers started firing at us, though we were at least 700 yards away. We could hear the gunfire and heard bullets flying by as we reached the tunnel leading to the cave entrance, but no one was hit. Thankfully, the land mines slowed the progress enough that our lead was preserved and kept them out of firing range. Ethan was now a few hundred yards away from the tunnel but the gunfire had stopped, and no pursuer was close to him. We entered the tunnel and made our way towards the cave knowing Ethan was now safe.

Once we reached the tunnel, everyone started to calm down but Faith. She was acting erratically and emotional, and was outwardly anxious. I went back to try to calm her but it was to no avail. Holly tried and it did not work. I decided to go ahead and get the TNT charge ready for detonation to close the tunnel off to assure our safety after everyone safely entered. There was no time to set any booby traps. I was about two minutes ahead of Holly and the kids, who each walked quickly down the passage, past the steel door, to the cave entrance. Though we had practiced this dozens of times, the terror of the moment made everyone anxious. This was not a scenario we had practiced and it didn't seem real.

I readied the detonator and was ready to trigger as one by one Adam, Faith, Grace and Holly followed each other towards me. As they approached where I was positioned, Faith abruptly cut and pushed past Adam, tripping directly onto the detonator. Her thigh triggered the explosion before Ethan could enter the cave. For all we knew, the explosion buried Ethan in dirt in the now closed passage to the cave entrance.

No words can describe the feelings that ran through my mind at that moment. I exchanged a look with Faith, who was frozen with shock, and then at Holly, who stared at me before closing her eyes and silently shedding tears for the only time I had ever seen in my life.

Anger, despair, emptiness, and letting Andrea down all raced through my mind before I realized Ethan could possibly be stuck outside. Everyone sat in total silence and shock except for Faith, who was hysterically crying while being held by Holly and Grace. I immediately left everyone and raced to the periscope to try to see if I could see Ethan. Nothing could have prepared me for what I saw next.

Chapter 9

Life through a Periscope

What followed was worse than I ever could have imagined. Looking through the periscope, I saw that about two dozen men had broken through and were hovering around the house. They were armed and angry.

After watching the men wandering around for few minutes, I saw the most bitter-sweet sight of my life. Ethan was alive but was being held at gunpoint by two men on his way down the mountain towards the house. When the men took him down to the house, he was surrounded by the entire gang. I couldn't breathe as I watched Ethan get struck in the stomach, causing him to fall to his knees. I could see that Ethan and the bikers were in a heated conversation, led by the biker that had asked me for directions that first day. I was sure I was going to see Ethan being executed, but the conversation continued for a while. Luckily, Ethan was helped up by some of the bikers. He led the group to a bomb shelter we had built as insurance in case something happened to the cave or we couldn't safely reach the cave. I let out a large sigh of relief that they didn't kill Ethan, guessing he bargained his life for assuring the gang's safety in the bomb shelter. The bomb shelter was stocked with several months of food for up to 20 people, with thousands of gallons of fresh water.

The combination of Ethan about to live with this angry mob with such little experience with others terrified me. He was in danger, we were in danger, and I was not there to protect him. I contemplated going through the water passage to save him, but then both of us would never get back.

With the premature triggering of the explosion, all our plans literally blew up on us. Our safety, my promise to keep the boys safe I'd made to Andrea by finding and preparing the cave, and Ethan's and Faith's union all were seemingly wiped away.

The next 60 days were the longest, darkest days of my life as I stared into the periscope every waking minute. There was no longer a blue sky. Everything looked cold, dark, and gray. There was a hazy look to the sky. There was no sign of activity in the house. I hoped and prayed that Ethan would be smart enough to stay alive using the shelter and the survival skills that we had learned.

Everything we had hoped for in the cave was turned upside down. We hoped for a calm and safe family life. Instead we got a mix of confusion, guilt, fear, stress, and loss. I didn't hear anyone, ignored Faith, was distant from Holly, and really only spoke to Adam about different options to rescue Ethan and bring him back.

After a few days, Adam insisted on taking shifts with me watching through the periscope when I was sleeping or eating, and that's how we spent our days. I blamed myself entirely for what happened. I could have refused to let him save his lizard. Faith's triggering the explosion was an accident, and it should have been me if anyone was left outside. I was extremely depressed and felt helpless. It was as though my body was stuck in the cave and my soul was with Ethan, trying to bring him back safely to us. For the rest of my life, I've blamed myself for what happened with Ethan.

About 70 days after we entered the cave, Adam saw Ethan and the rest of the group emerge from the shelter. There was about 20 men and women preparing to leave the property. Adam ran to get me, but by the time I got there, all I could see was Ethan getting into a gray, snow-covered vehicle along with the rest of the people, loaded with a bunch of water and boxes.

Talk about feeling emptiness in your life. My son Ethan was forced to fight for survival during nuclear winter on Earth, while being exposed to radiation, with a group of armed bikers, instead of being safe and secure in our cave like we had planned for so many years. I cried for hours every day knowing that this was likely the last time I would ever see him, again wishing I could take his place.

It's hard to describe the feeling of losing a child, especially to anyone who hasn't had one. It is not the way things are supposed to happen in nature. Losing Andrea was like being hit by a truck; losing Ethan was the same, or worse. It was not a disease that hit him. It was an error I'd made, and now my son was in the exact environment I'd fought for years to keep him out of.

Ethan not being with us cast a cloud over our plans for the cave. Faith and Ethan were supposed to be a couple, as were Grace and Adam, in order to repopulate the world after its destruction. The whole dynamic and mood shifted. My distance from Holly and Faith didn't help the atmosphere in the cave

Ethan, being out there unprotected in the middle of a long nuclear winter, made me think a lot more about the billions out there whose lives ended, or would soon end, from the aftereffects of the nuclear bombs. A damaged water supply, shorter growing seasons, lack of medicine, and radiation were all factors leading to man's pending extinction. I don't think I would have thought about them as much if Ethan was with us. It was depressing, mind-boggling, and highly upsetting to think about, but my mind went there on a daily basis.

Each person deals with loss differently. Holly remained strong and determined to create as stable an environment as we could have. Adam was devastated by his missing twin. They had shared everything throughout their lives and had never been apart. Grace felt bad for everyone, and truly missed the bond the four kids shared.

Faith, unbelievably, was gaining faith, and kept the most positive outlook. She said she knew Ethan could rise to any challenge and that she was certain he would make it back to her so they could share their lives. I smiled at her when she expressed her optimistic view, but inside, I felt pity for her, as I strongly doubted anyone could survive out there.

I was silent, depressed, and only allowed myself hope once a day when I would go to the periscope in the morning through lunchtime to see if there were any signs of activity. Usually, I had to ask Faith, who spent countless hours peering out the periscope, to let me look for a while. I saw nothing, visualizing a world without food, fresh water, and no peaceful living. It was a world where man had lost any semblance of the civilized man he thought he was. I spent the next seven months gazing through the periscope, desperate for a sign of Ethan. I lost more and more hope and faith each day that passed that I didn't see Ethan.

After seven months from the time I saw Ethan leave, I decided it was best to not stare out the periscope for hours each day. I was depressed and unfocused on my family inside the cave. I turned my attention to the people in the cave. This was very hard on me at first. I found myself unfocused, distracted, and often thinking about Ethan.

In private, Holly and I spoke about what to do about Faith. We spoke about the potential of Adam also mating with Faith. It was a strange and hard topic to discuss. We felt that we needed to consider that Faith would be depressed if Adam and Grace had children. We didn't bring up anything at this point, but prepared ourselves for the conversations that would need to happen with all the kids on this subject.

About 10 months after we entered the cave, we noticed that Faith still spent most of her days staring out the periscope. She said she felt that Ethan was coming back and she wanted to be the one who saw him first. I pitied her more than ever. I was losing more hope every day while she was gaining faith every day.

When I did look outside, the world looked different. The snow did not leave the ground in the summer like it had all the other years. Everything was gray and dark. There was no sign of animals or humans. After 11 months I stopped looking for Ethan and gave up all hope he survived.

It was about a year after we came into the cave that I awoke one night and walked to the restroom area. Before coming back to bed, I decided to walk down and look through the periscope. I don't know what I was expecting to see, but I decided to peer around for a minute.

I froze in a combination of fear, exhilaration, and anticipation when I saw a lantern shining inside the house. My heart raced as I could see a figure but couldn't make out who it was. I ran the few hundred yards back to the main cave to wake Adam in what seemed to be seconds. I couldn't breathe or speak when I woke him. I was out of shape and hyperventilating. Scared I was dying, Adam woke everyone, and Holly tried to give me mouth to mouth. I finally caught my breath and told them someone was in the house.

Faith disappeared in a millisecond like a sprinter. A couple of minutes later, as we approached the periscope, Faith screamed with elation, "Its Ethan." I don't know how she could have been so sure. I saw the bearded, ragged figure seemingly looking directly in our direction, pointing at his heart and making thumbs up and hugging motions. When Faith explained that that was their secret code, we all broke down into a group crying session before planning a rescue mission.

The only way to save Ethan was very risky and dangerous. We knew we could go downstream to the lake, but had no idea what coming back would entail. We fought over who would go through the underwater canal with spare tanks and gear to get Ethan. Faith wanted to go but we eventually decided Adam and I would go; Faith was upset that she couldn't come. I felt bad telling Faith she couldn't come, knowing she blamed herself for Ethan being locked out. She wanted redemption, but Holly and I felt Adam and I were best fit for the job.

I had brought two handguns into the cave in case of emergency and decided to take them with us in case we encountered any problems. I hoped that I was being overly paranoid that we would encounter the gang. I packed the guns in a waterproof bag and put it into my wetsuit.

Adam and I readied ourselves in our scuba gear and set out down to the underwater passageway. Before leaving, we fastened a 200-foot-long rope around a rock and told Holly, Faith, and Grace that they should pull the rope when we come back to help us through the current.

We each had underwater lights, three oxygen tanks, and extra scuba gear for Ethan as we made our way down the long dark canal. We encountered three areas which were very narrow and claustrophobic, but we managed to squeeze through it. Under any other circumstance besides saving my son, I would have turned back. Carl was wrong. This was extreme for a lifelong caver, let alone a middle-aged, out-of-shape rank amateur, but none of that mattered. After about 45 minutes and three-quarters of a full oxygen tank each, we made it to the lake. My first thought was thank God we brought extra tanks, because the way back would be twice as hard and we may run out of oxygen.

As we emerged from the lake and breathed our first breaths outside the cave, I felt nauseous. There was a terrible smell you could taste in your mouth; I could not imagine what it was like for Ethan to breathe this for a year. As we made our way to the house, we were reunited with Ethan. Even today, the way he looked is etched in my mind and haunts me; I still physically shudder at the thought of his appearance. His face and hands were blistered. He had lost a lot of weight. He was disheveled, weak, disoriented, but very much alive and happy to be reunited with us.

He looked like someone who had been through hell on earth. As I hugged him, I wondered where the Ethan I knew was and what had happened to him. It felt like it was a first hug with a new Ethan.

We had brought food, water, and a concoction of medications Holly had put together. He was having a hard time speaking, and couldn't catch his breath to explain what happened. He told us that he had witnessed mankind's lowest level, and that we should get moving back because he was sure two men named Thump and Bear would come to track him down when they discovered what happened. We worried that Ethan was delirious, but heeded his advice.

I hurried to ready the gear as Adam readied Ethan and helped him get in the suit. I decided to give Adam one of the guns in case Ethan was right about the men tracking him. Before we left, I told Adam I was worried we would run out of oxygen before we made it into the cave and that if I flashed my light on and off twice in the water passage, he needed to go ahead without me and Ethan to get extra oxygen tanks in case we were running low. The plan to help Ethan return against the current was to surround him on both sides and push him with us.

After successfully getting Ethan into the gear, we decided to make out way to the lake. As we opened the door to leave the house, two men were standing at the entrance. They looked like two wolves and were pacing menacingly back and forth in front of us. They were not holding guns, but they seemed even more dangerous due to their animalistic behavior. One of the men was older and yelling—or more like hissing—at Ethan for betraying them. The younger one pulled out a large hunting knife. At this moment I felt the most fear I had ever felt in my life. I froze for a second, believing that none of us would make it back to the cave.

As a father my first impulse was to protect my kids by any means necessary. I was against violence and killing, but I thought that the only way to survive was to pull out my gun and shoot them. Before pulling my gun, I looked at them and thought about what they had gone through and what the nuclear winter was doing to them. They were living their last days and they knew it. I didn't know what to do. On one hand, they were threatening our lives and might attack. On the other hand, their actions were made out of fear for their own lives and safety. In the last second, I decided to appeal to their survival instincts. Instead of pulling my gun and shooting them, I simply asked them if they wanted food and water. Surprised by this offer, they remarkably seemed to gather themselves and were intrigued by the offer. After not verbally responding to my initial offer, I calmly asked them to back away and let us go in peace. They seemed to get more agitated and hostile again as they hissed incoherently about betrayal, Ethan, and orders. I was again conflicted because I saw some level of reason and survival instincts when I mentioned food, but they were getting angry as time passed. , Set on not turning to violence, I decided to try my ways one last time. I offered to send fresh fish and other food to help them survive , if they would let us go. I saw from their reactions that we had the makings of a deal. We agreed that we would give the food and water we had with is immediately. Then they would leave the property and drive a mile away to give us time to make our way back into the cave. In exchange, we would send them lots of food and water down the water passageway in two to three hours. It was a win-win agreement, through dialogue, that avoided pulling out a gun and killing them. As they ate the food we brought with us, the men broke down and started to cry. I thought about how many more survivors were still living like these men.

I was thankful we didn't have to use the guns, which was part of the technology I wish was never developed. The problem with guns and weapons were that there were simply too many people who were willing to use them. Man was quite simply a species where certain individuals and leaders were willing to use weapons to kill others for no valid reason.

I could only imagine what Holly and the girls thought watching this from the cave. With my stress level just settling down to only extremely elevated, and the two men off our property, we made our way to the water. Ethan didn't look good at all. I wondered about even starting in his condition, but that was not an option. We planned that Adam and I each would use one and a quarter tanks on the way back and keep two tanks for Ethan.

The swimming was tough at first. The current and Ethan's weakness made our progress very slow. I was worried that we wouldn't make it back. It was hard for me, let alone Ethan. I don't know how it happened, but whether it was the water, or the pure oxygen, or the thought that Faith was there at the end of this journey, Ethan did well through the middle sections. However, despite our progress, we were running low on oxygen. We were about two-thirds of the way back when I gave Adam the signal to go on with two flashes. Up until then, Adam and I were each holding Ethan on one side and we made good time. Adam still had a half a tank, as did I. Ethan had used one full tank and was starting his second.

The minute Adam left, we began to slow down. Ethan was weak and I lost Adam's help. My mind started to race with the thought of losing Ethan twice. I garnered all my strength and pushed forward for about fifteen minutes, but my tank emptied and Ethan and I had to share the last tank, which was now half full. The situation was critical. I wanted Ethan to survive more than I cared about living. I started to panic. We wouldn't make it back without Adam coming back with new tanks. I was scared for our lives.

In the midst of my fear and anxiety, with the last tank now empty, a flash of white light appeared before my eyes. I kept thinking: Was this the end? Was this the white light that people who had died and come back had described?

As the white light drew closer, I saw what appeared to be a seal swimming toward us, it looked like the same seal that swum up to the glass during my first kiss with Andrea. I couldn't help but think about Andrea and how I failed her. As this seal approached us, I regained my focus and, to my surprise, it was actually Faith who had swum down with two extra oxygen tanks. There was no predicting or stopping Faith. She was the most welcome sights Ethan and I had ever seen.

After a moment when Faith and Ethan looked into each other's eyes, in a moment of true emotion where her look of love, sorrow, and concern at what he had been through could be interpreted through her expression, we made our way back. Adam came down to help the final 10 percent of the way. When we all finally emerged, we were whole again. The relief and joy we felt at being whole again is hard to express. It was a moment of unity I will never forget.

The moment of joy was brief. Ethan looked horrible and vomited out everything in his stomach, including some blood. Faith, Grace, and Holly immediately began the work on Ethan's recovery. Adam and I went to gather food and fish to send to Thump and Bear, as we had promised, and then went to help out with Ethan's long recovery.

Chapter 10

Mankind's Low

Ethan was incoherent for a few days. We mostly kept him covered in warm, wet towels from the spring with occasional baths that became more frequent as his condition improved. He couldn't keep any food down besides for white rice and water, so we nursed him on that for a month until he began to tolerate other foods. He rapidly lost what remained of his hair during his first week in the cave. He threw up for weeks as he battled the effects of radiation. Holly told me she was worried that he could have become sterile from the radiation exposure. We found out later why these things happened to him upon his return to our cave.

Faith barely left his side. She was constantly asking Holly about what to do to help Ethan and demanded she be in charge of everything. She was, if I may say so, transformed, showing fewer examples of her former chaotic nature. The setting and united family from Ethan's return had a calming effect on her.

Three months after his rescue, Ethan asked us to assemble after dinner one night to tell us everything that happened to him outside the cave for the first time since his return. Ethan knew we wanted to hear what he went through but no one pressured him. We knew he had nightmares, so we gave him his space allowing him to tell us what happened only when he was ready. Listening to his story was the possibly longest and hardest three hours of my life and it still haunts me. Below is Ethan's story of what happened during his year away from us.

***

Ethan had been about a hundred feet from the passageway when the explosives detonated that sealed the cave. At first, he didn't know what to do or what had happened. After gathering his thoughts, he realized that the bomb shelter was the only safe place for him regardless of having to face the intruders. He encountered two armed men halfway down the mountain, who led him down to the gang in front of the house.

At the house, the gang's leader, Mike "Caveman" Fowler, used his club to knock the wind out of Ethan, sending him to the ground. He told Ethan he was going to club him to death to pay us back for the men he'd lost from the land mines if Ethan didn't tell him how to get access to the cave. Ethan responded that that he couldn't get in himself and that no one could get close to the cave without setting off the traps. He added that Caveman would just have to kill him if accessing the cave was his only goal. Ethan was smart though. He told the men that we had built a bomb shelter in case the cave didn't work out and that their survival from the radiation enveloping the world depended on him being alive.

Ethan told them how he had been studying how to survive in adverse conditions, could access food and shelter to protect the gang for months, and would be an asset to Caveman if he spared his life. Caveman listened to Ethan and agreed to spare him, but only after telling Ethan that if he ever crossed him in any way, shape, or form he would club him to death.

Ethan led 12 men and 6 women to the bomb shelter we had built. There, Ethan learned that the Hell's Rejects made about $10,000,000 per year from its business activities and had split into four groups, to try to ensure that some survived Doomsday. Caveman was decorated ex-military who wanted to live life as if everyone was involved in a war for survival. He got what he wanted—until the global nuclear war killed billions.

Caveman was built like a bull and as strong as one too. No one messed with him. He carried a wooden club he'd carved himself, exactly like one carried by cavemen, which he used to hurt or kill people, display power and control, and knock girls out who refused his unwanted advances. This symbol of male superiority, which goes back to the images of cavemen, showed how some men had come full circle He was a bully and a pig of a man, but Ethan figured out how to appeal to his survival instincts to stay alive.

In the bomb shelter, Ethan tried to keep to himself, but it was impossible. Caveman was so thankful for being safe and underground that he decided to make Ethan vice president of the gang, replacing the former vice president who was killed by a land mine entering our property. Ethan was reluctant at first, but Caveman insisted, so Ethan and the others all fell in line with his wishes.

The bomb shelter was a den of corruption. The club members would have sex with their partners in front of everyone and do drugs all day, every day. They even tried to take Ethan's virginity when one of the women, Cherry, a hefty, purple haired lass with 30 body piercings, jumped him as he was sleeping, while the club members held him down after he woke. Caveman stopped this act by clubbing Cherry over the head, causing the others to back off. This act by Caveman showed Ethan how he was important to him and dispensable he was without his protection.

Ethan learned to keep his true thoughts to himself. He told himself that Caveman was an evil man but that he needed to stay close to him and serve him as a leader to survive until he could make his escape. Ethan knew that his place was in our cave and that he had to make sure the club members never had a chance to hurt us. Ethan began plotting his escape within hours of entering the bomb shelter.

Ethan impressed the gang with his knowledge of nuclear war survival procedures. He explained there was a short-term plan to get underground with safe food and water as they had done, and then to emerge and establish long-term supplies of fresh water and food in an altered world with undetermined damage.

No one knew how many bombs had been launched, but one club member they called Beast had served on nuclear subs and said if the US was under attack, his sub would have launched at least 30 missiles themselves. They were one of 50 nuclear subs. The thought of the damage that could have been caused if every country fired their missiles was frightening. Mankind could be lucky to survive a week or two if thousands of warheads were delivered around the world.

During the second month in the shelter, as supplies dwindled, Caveman instructed Ethan to prepare an exit plan for the club. Ethan organized the remaining food, personal care, and water and boxed all the supplies to move to the next stop, which was Cheyenne, where the other club members were supposed to meet up after Doomsday. Before leaving, Ethan had the club members fill a few hundred gallons of water from the lake, even though it had been exposed to radiation. Ethan figured the radiated water was diluted from the flow from our springs in the cave. He also had the club members fill up their motorcycles and truck with fuel before they left.

Ethan stressed to the club members that they were going to be exposed to radiation, and that it was important to travel to their next destination at light-speed to get back underground with supplies. A safe food supply was of great concern to Ethan and the club ahead of their exit. Caveman heeded Ethan's warnings and put great trust in his words.

Ethan relayed to us how hard it was to leave the property with his future in doubt, but knew that our survival was at stake if the club members stayed. He had told the club members that we had set up automatic weapons that could be remote-control-operated (though this was not true) and had set all sorts of traps, making entry impossible. He also pushed everyone to forget about the cave and prepare for survival in nuclear winter with the others in Cheyenne as planned.

When Ethan and the club arrived to Cheyenne, they found the town deserted. They didn't know if people were dead, hiding, or had fled to warmer places. It was freezing, so they made their way to the most expensive areas in town and went door to door to see if there were any homes with bomb shelters. They found a large, deep earth shelter built by Atlas Survival Shelters after about two hours of searching.

What followed were episodes of barbarism and inhumanity that would haunt Ethan, and the rest of us, for years. It was then that he knew he had to plan and execute a way to kill Caveman and try to make it back to us. When he saw what they did to the family in the shelter, he understood what would have happened to all of us if Caveman had a chance to access our cave.

Caveman instructed the club to force open the bomb shelter hatch and kick everyone in the shelter out. Two families, totaling 10 people, had been surviving in the shelter. Among them were two young ladies in their early twenties that attracted Caveman, so he ordered the girls back into the shelter and demanded the remaining family members to leave and never come back. When the two fathers fought Caveman's orders, their whole families were executed on the spot. Caveman clubbed each member over the head before Beast shot them in the back of their heads with a .44-caliber handgun. Unfazed, as if nothing happened, Caveman pushed the hysterical girls down the stairs into the shelter and the rest of the biker club and Ethan followed.

As Ethan continued his story, I could see Holly's face tighten as she heard what happened to the young girls. Upon the group getting underground into the shelter, Caveman tried to escort both of girls into one of the built-in bedrooms. When the girls refused and tried to fight him off, Caveman lightly knocked each one in the head with his wooden club and then dragged the half-unconscious girls by the hair into the room, where he had his way with them. After he was satisfied, Caveman then offered the girls to the other club members and Ethan, who was the only one not to partake in their acts of rape.

Later that night, two loud gunshots woke everyone. As the gang walked towards the sound, they found the two girls lying on the ground with holes in their temples and blood pouring out of their heads. Next to them were two guns and a suicide note which cursed Caveman and the group to an eternity in Hell. Caveman laughed, saying Satan already kicked him out of Hell, and went right back to sleep.

In the new shelter, Ethan was charged with taking inventory, making the living conditions as good as possible, and keeping all assets organized and located. Ethan worked for Caveman, assisting in keeping track of the club's missions that club members were assigned to; each member was assigned to a mission that required them to exit the shelter It was not easy for Ethan to work for Caveman, but he kept his thoughts 100 percent private and told himself Caveman's trust in him would lead to an opportunity for his escape back to our cave.

Club members were sent out on missions wearing one of the three shared radiation suits from our shelter to find out what happened, who survived, and where they were. Some were out for hours, others days. The suits and riding motorcycles did not go well together; most of the suits were compromised, leading to radiation exposure.

Caveman and Ethan never left the shelter. The others rotated their missions. Beast was in charge of bringing all of the club's buried assets to the shelter. That included gold, diamonds, platinum, silver, fuel, cash (though that seemed useless), and a vast cache of weapons. Upon seeing the variety of weaponry that Hell's Rejects had purchased, Ethan knew we made a mistake threatening the club with our land mines. The Hell's Rejects could win a war in a small country with the money, weapons, and explosives they had. Business had been good, allowing Caveman to build a small army with no one able to stop his growth.

The reports that started coming in were hard to digest. The US and Russia had launched over 500 nuclear warheads at each other. Over 1,200 warheads were detonated globally. The world's ideal of brotherhood was replaced with an attitude that said, "If we are going down, so are you". No one could have predicted this immense volume of radiation encompassing the Earth. Big cities were flattened by multiple warheads. Blast victims were either surviving underground or died on the surface. Only those with shelters and enough supplies could assure short term survival.

Approximately 95–100 percent of all people living in the biggest cities died immediately or from radiation exposure within days of Doomsday. 100 percent of people without bomb shelters globally were dead within days. There were pockets of survivors outside the big cities, but the life expectancy for those exposed to radiation was only a couple of months. Thousands of shelters had been purchased from companies like Atlas as things worsened globally, but few, if any, were meant to last for 40 years. Coming out before it was safe meant death. People stayed in their shelters as long as they could. Once they emerged they faced an invisible enemy armed with the invasive ability to eliminate every living species on the surface.

Ethan estimated there was six to seven months' worth of safe food and water in the shelter. There was no fresh food or water on the surface, according to the reports that were coming in. All the money in the world could not buy you an uncontaminated bottle of water on the Earth's surface.

Within weeks of entering the shelter, most of the inhabitants, including Ethan, began showing signs of radiation exposure. Those going on missions started losing their hair. All had diarrhea, nausea, or bloody vomiting. Beast's cousin Bluto, who had been one of the bikers who spent days outside with a compromised radiation suit, suffered a seizure and died. The group was frightened, many for the first time in their adult lives.

Knowing that the group was suffering from mild radiation sickness and a lowered ability to fight infection, Ethan advised Caveman that each member should keep to themselves and not exchange bodily fluids. Ethan was doing better than most, having kept his hair, and only suffered from diarrhea and vomiting for a couple weeks.

The day-to-day life in the shelter became routine. Ethan continued to keep to himself, besides for his daily reporting and advice sessions with Caveman. Those too became routine, since the plan was to do nothing for the next four months except ration food to make it last longer. Caveman pushed Ethan to figure out how to make the food last for a full year.

Ethan learned to resent everything Caveman stood for. Seemingly every other sentence from Caveman put down blacks, Mexicans, homosexuals, Jews, or Asians. His prize possession was an old Nazi biker's helmet with a swastika on it. Every time he held that helmet he said that the Nazis knew how to keep order and treat Jews, Gypsies, and gays. The swastika on his helmet was matched with a massive tattooed swastika on his back. Ethan contemplated whether Caveman had in fact known Satan and if Satan actually kicked him out of Hell for being too evil. He was full of hate and violence, demonstrating an absolute absence of humanity on Earth. Ethan would nod in agreement with everything Caveman said, while his brain searched for a way to kill him and escape back to our cave.

The bikers became anxious and stir-crazy over the next few months. People in the shelter were losing weight rapidly, bored from being confined and staying away from personal contact. Bikers still went on scouting missions, with some going out for a week or two before coming back. The bikers who went out continued to come back with mild radiation sickness. The only report that came in claimed that survivors were planning to meet in California's Central Valley, which was known for its fertile farmland. The person who reported this to the bikers spoke of California as if it were paradise. It sounded too good to be true to Caveman, who advised the members to forget about it.

Regardless of the threat to their lives by radiation, one of the couples and two of the male bikers in the shelter decided they were going to leave for California. They made their way in the middle of the night with about 25 percent of the gang's food and all the fuel they could carry. They had told one of the remaining members that they were going crazy underground and were going to try to make it to the California farming valley, where they were originally from. Upon discovering they'd gone, Caveman was furious and left the shelter for the first time since they'd arrived in Cheyenne to try to catch them, taking Beast with him.

Two days passed before Caveman and Beast came back. They caught the escapees300 miles from Cheyenne. Caveman had the heads of the four former members tied to the back of his motorcycle. He had dragged them the whole ride back. Every person in the shelter, especially Ethan, learned from the message Caveman delivered; nobody messes with Caveman.

Within a day after they returned, Caveman and Beast started feeling the effects of radiation sickness. Caveman was vomiting blood, Beast battling diarrhea. Both lost all their hair within days. It had been about six months since Doomsday and the surface was not even close to being safe. Beast died in the middle of the night a week after returning from the chase. Caveman had the look of a man beaten for the first time in his life. Fear of the invisible enemy lurking outside grew every day.

The gang was down to eight men and five women, including Ethan. Caveman was still sick. Even with Caveman slowed by radiation sickness, the others were afraid of him, especially after he strolled in with the four members' heads. The bikers who still went out on scouting missions had experienced some level of brain damage and were not speaking clearly anymore.

After eight months in the shelter, the daily meeting focused on what the Hell's Rejects would do when food and water in the shelter ran out. They had three months of rationed food left. Caveman was focused on going back to where he was born in Mississippi, thinking that the fewest bombs exploded there, water was available, and the land was fertile. He understood that there was a possibility they could all die. He also thought that any place they came to that was able to sustain life would be the spot they would settle in. Ethan agreed to his plan, and started preparations for packing and transferring assets. They were going to leave in 60 days.

It was 45 days later, at a daily meeting, where Caveman noticed Ethan daydreaming. When he asked Ethan what he was thinking of, Ethan panicked and said he was thinking about planning the trip. Caveman noticed this tiny moment as an irregularity and started pressing Ethan on whether he was thinking about his family and our cave. Ethan told him no, but Caveman kept asking him at the daily meetings about whether they could enter our cave.

Ethan told us how he looked Caveman right in the eyes and lied to him, saying that I was a master at building bombs, setting traps, and that I had used all my talents to protect the cave from intruders. Ethan also pushed back asking Caveman if he thought he would have come out to face him if there was a way into the cave.

Caveman did not relent. He asked if Ethan knew where the traps were. Could he navigate through the traps to gain access to the tunnel? He wanted to blast his way in. Each refusal or denial started frustrating Caveman. Finally, Ethan told him he had done everything Caveman asked, and helped him survive by making sure to always provide his best advice. He told Caveman he was 100 percent certain that going southeast toward the Mississippi River was their best bet when they emerged. Ethan told him the cave was certain death.

The questioning made Ethan nervous. He knew he had to plan his escape soon and do it in such a way as to prevent Caveman and the gang from chasing him. He did not want his head on the back of Caveman's motorcycle. In the days leading up to the gang's journey to Mississippi, Ethan created his plan.

A few days before the Hell's Rejects were supposed to leave as a group, Ethan overheard two of the members, Thump and Bear, who were about to leave on a scouting mission, talking about Caveman's plan of going back to our cave and blasting their way in. Ethan could not make out every word they were saying, but it sounded like Ethan was actually packing for Hell's Rejects to go back to our cave to try to gain access without him knowing it. Ethan now needed to accelerate his plan to protect himself and all of us in the cave.

Ethan enacted his plan that night. He woke up three in the morning while everyone was sleeping and executed a plan that could only be justified by knowing he was protecting us and the cave. Ethan had readied all of the gang's supplies near the entrance of the shelter. His plan was to start a massive fire that would consume all of the supplies and ignite the explosives, killing the gang members in the shelter. He made sure the water would not be reachable by placing it closest to the entrance.

To enact this plan, Ethan decided that he would start a fire using Caveman's wooden club by soaking it and the supplies in kerosene. He would also create a trail of gunpowder leading to the explosives, which would ignite after he escaped. Additionally, he planned to seal the only exit to the shelter to prevent any of the members inside from escaping.

Ethan lit the fire without being noticed, making sure it spread quickly. Once the supplies were on fire, he raced out of the shelter and sealed it shut. Once outside, Ethan filled up Caveman's Harley Davidsons with fuel. He started driving away and was 50 yards from the shelter when he stopped to look back. He heard faint cries emanating from the shelter preceding a massive explosion that shook the ground and resulted in a peaceful silence. Ethan said he felt as if the explosion kicked something awful back to the depths of the Earth's fiery core.

Ethan started back towards our cave on Caveman's Harley and made it a ways past Thermopolis when the Thump and Bear, who were coming back from their scouting mission, passed him coming the other way. Noticing Caveman's motorcycle, they turned around and caught up to Ethan, who did not try to evade them. Ethan told them that he had packed everything and spoke to Caveman, who decided they should all try to access the cave. He told the men that Caveman wanted him to start laying down a safe path up the mountain and that Caveman and the rest of the members were joining him in a couple of days. Suspicious of Ethan, and knowing that Caveman had just sent them to scout the property, the two men decided that one of them would stay with Ethan while the other went back to check on his story.

Before the one man left, Ethan excused himself to go into the woods to go to the bathroom. Ethan hung his jacket up on a bush and squatted down about 30 yards from the members, who were talking incoherently. It occurred to them Ethan was taking a long time, so they both approached his jacket. When they got to his jacket, they saw that Ethan was gone, and the only way to chase him was on foot, which they were not going to do. They took the keys out of the Harley and drove back to Cheyenne to see what Caveman wanted to do, knowing where Ethan was headed.

Ethan was 40 miles from our cave and was weak. He had no food, because he had to leave it in the Harley, and only four bottles of water that he had strapped on his back under his radiation suit. Over the next two days, Ethan walked back to our property, where we executed our rescue mission to bring Ethan back to the cave.

At the end of Ethan's story, we all sat in a silence, digesting what we'd just heard. Ethan had saved our lives by overhearing Caveman's plot. He had seen the worst behavior mankind was capable of and had firsthand knowledge of how billions of people were killed. As I sat there, thinking what happened to my son, I felt like I'd failed in protecting him from one of the future forces of evil Andrea and I saw coming. I should have been the one to suffer in the outside world. I have never forgiven myself for what happened to Ethan.

Chapter 11

Living in Noah's Cave

It was clear to me that the Earth's natural defense system would eliminate the species that damaged it and regenerate without the interference of man. I was outside the cave for a few hours; it took me weeks to feel normal again. The Earth was not a place for man during this rebirth. Time and patience were the only paths that could lead to the planet's rebirth and ability to deliver conditions where man could survive. The only question was how long it would take. We asked Grace and Faith to record the annual changes to the environment to observe how long it would take for things to look normal.

It took Ethan over three years to recover from the radiation exposure. Holly was fairly sure he was going to have long-term problems. The healing powers of the water helped, but the permanent damage was severe. Holly's medical experience was invaluable. We had brought as many medical supplies as we could to cover as many different diseases or conditions as possible.

Ethan was physically scarred for life. Thankfully, he was fully healed mentally. Thinking about what happened to him still brings a sickening feeling of guilt to the pit of my stomach. The joy at having him back is always tempered with my wish it had happened to me instead. No parent can stand thinking of the bad things that happen to their child.

Ethan's driving force for recovery was Faith. Faith was amazing during his recovery. She somehow was calm, focused, patient, caring, and quite a wonder to see. I felt bad for thinking about thinking she was chaotic, as she was everything but chaotic here. She was the perfect caring partner for Ethan and they operated as one, the way Andrea and I used to. Somehow, I think the closed environment and a singular purpose were good for Faith. She knew her role and excelled in it. I remember thinking that she was invaded or influenced by Andrea's soul as I watched her develop from the depths of blaming herself for Ethan's unfortunate ordeal to becoming his devoted partner.

The early years after Ethan came back were the most peaceful years in the cave. Everyone had a job and a routine. Everyone had a significant other. There was plenty of time and places for family time, couple time, and alone time for each of us.

Adam and Grace were the steady, dependable couple you know you can count on through thick and thin. Grace was quiet, loving, nurturing, and smart, but there was something distant in her eyes from time to time. She didn't show her cards or emotions and was not as public with her affection. Adam was a natural leader, good-looking, inventive, and quick-witted. He was also a bit emotionally disconnected. He was strong, happy-go-lucky, and was relieved to have Ethan back.

In the months after Ethan came back, I realized what a terrible job I had done during the year he was gone. It was like I was in a period of mourning before he was dead. It was unfair to everyone, but mostly to Holly, who couldn't tell me what a bad job I was doing. She didn't want to hurt my feelings. Holly herself felt bad that Faith made a mistake.

I apologized to Holly and everyone for how things started at one of our weekly family discussion where, depending on the mood, we spoke about what happened to the world, our life and purpose in the cave, and our plan for what we would do when we emerged from the cave.

It was right after our fourth year in the cave that Holly said she thought it would be a good time for the kids to be joined ceremoniously. It was already assumed that they were pairs and it was time to make it official. We decided to hold a surprise wedding for them the following week.

Holly did everything for the ceremony. I prepared the food the night before while everyone slept. When it was time for our weekly discussion, Holly asked the girls to go with her to talk in private. I asked the boys help get some things and then had them both go bathe and get dressed in their best clothes, while Holly had the girls get dressed while she did their hair. Neither of us told them what was happening, though they pestered us with questions, predicting it was for a surprise wedding ceremony.

We had them stay in place for thirty minutes while Holly decorated the area on the edge of the spring with a white cloth pad and a runway decorated with a couple dozen flashlights highlighting several rows of floral arches which created a hundred-foot quarter-circle runway leading to the spring.

If you are lucky enough to have attended wedding ceremonies of various cultures and religions, you will know that there is great beauty in every culture's wedding ceremony. If you could have taken the love and beauty of every religion's and culture's wedding ceremony and spread that around the world instead of the hate and chaos, maybe the end would not have come.

At the ceremony, I stood by the spring with the urn containing Andrea's remains on a table covered with a white tablecloth, while Holly got the kids, confirmed this was their wedding ceremony, and choreographed them walking down the aisle. I don't know how she did it, but Holly made the girls look like they just got out of the best hairstyle salon. They were carrying bouquets and were wearing medium-length white dresses and veils. Knowing this ceremony was Andrea's plan gave me a sense of great relief due to the journey we'd taken to get to this point in time.

We decided to have a somber and hopeful ceremony that touched on all the topics of our weekly meetings. Holly and I were going to speak to them about where they came from, where they were, where they were going, and how they needed to work as one with each other to reach the goal of what was to come.

We started with a moment of silence to honor and remember everyone who had been lost by the events that led us to the cave. I then spoke about Andrea and her role in making this moment possible. I reminded the kids about every precious person around the world who suffered and was lost in the nuclear war. I told them that by all rights, and without Andrea's plan, we should not be alive and sharing this moment. I finished with the thought of the kids having a future obligation to repopulate the world and learn from the mistakes of the past.

Holly took over and discussed the reality of where we were, how we didn't know how long we would be in the cave, and that it was up to them to fill the cave with kids and lead the next generation that would emerge from the cave. She told them that they would go through all sorts of things in life and that no matter what happened, they needed to deal with it calmly and in unison. She was emotional while speaking and gave the boys two rings for the girls; her mom's for Grace and Andrea's for Faith.

I explained that respect, reason, dialogue, and discussion need to succeed against impulse, nature, ego, and anger, or they will fail in the end. In conclusion, I said that mankind needs to establish a universal code of civilized conduct, without killing or hurting his fellow man. I charged them with preparing that code of conduct, teaching it to their children, and being living examples of that code.

The kids each took turns expressing their feelings for the other. While I can't remember the words they spoke because of the emotional roller coaster I was on, what I do remember was the look in my boys' eyes and the joy they had to be there with Grace and Faith. The love was apparent. Holly and I knew that each pair would be a lasting, devoted couple.

96

Following the wedding, Holly and I became much closer. Holly was matriarch, doctor, educator, and cook. I was the patriarch, farmer, fisherman, and inventory manager. We all had our jobs, supporting everything that needed to be done. The kids helped with all tasks.

We worked well as a group. We lived with a collective heartbeat, knowing our survival was linked together. No individual was more important than the other or the whole. As a result, a calm, respectful, and cooperative environment was created. The calm environment was the central goal of our life. It was a challenge to keep it, but each of us had to fight our impulses to be impatient, selfish, or insensitive.

Our day-to-day life was by no means exciting. We each had more than enough alone time and partners to spend intimate time with. We all had strong physical relationships and emotional bonds, which was very healthy, given there was no escaping anywhere. That said, I think everyone understood the gravity of what happened that left us needing the cave to survive and understood that decreasing chaos and the importance of the group rather than the self were the ideals we needed when we got a second chance to live on the surface.

The main thing that got monotonous was having few food choices. While we grew fruits and vegetables and farmed several types of freshwater fish, the bulk of our meals were pre-packed dried meals with 40- to 50-year shelf lives purchased from Wise Foods. We purchased hundreds of thousands of meat, chicken, and vegetable meals, mixing those with what we grew to keep nourished. It wasn't great, but it worked. By purchasing these meals, we didn't need to bring livestock down into the cave with us. We had purchased tons of dried milk, eggs, flour, and oats, and made great breakfasts. We ate every meal together unless one of us was sleeping. The food did get boring, but the alternative was being outside in the middle of a multi-decade-long nuclear winter.

Fishing was fun because we always caught a fish and it was a chance to have fun together, however, after 18, years it got a bit too easy. We released about half the fish, slowly, after about 15 years, for three reasons: one reason was to repopulate the lake and stream, the second was because I underestimated how fast they would reproduce, and the last reason was because I didn't buy enough fish food and didn't want to risk using any of our supplies to keep the fish fed.

***

The following years were hectic, to say the least. Grace and Adam had children in 2037, 2039, 2041, and 2043. Faith and Ethan had children in 2036, 2038, 2040, and 2044. Each had two boys and two girls. Babies and very young kids tend to be chaotic and always look for the most dangerous thing in the area to play with. There was no childproofing the areas we had to protect. The energy needed to manage a bunch of little kids running in opposite directions is something I can laugh at now, though it was a load until the older kids started maturing and began to help watch the little ones.

We decided it was time to begin our major project that we planned before entering the cave. In the spirit of the first cave dwellers and the history they provided in their paintings on the walls of caves, we commenced the painting of a massive canvas that we erected on the western wall of the cave. The painting was designed to tell the story of the ascent and fall of civilized man.

The painting started with a massive image of a clock. We wanted to show how mankind had come full circle back to needing caves to protect his survival. Every night after dinner we would work on the painting and teach the children about the rise and fall of humanity. The right side of the clock, from 12-6 o'clock, would depict the ascent of man from his beginnings using caves for protection. The left side, from 6-12 o'clock, would depict the downfall, leading to the full-circle story of civilized man. It was the most unfortunate of stories, leaving us as educated cavemen with the knowledge of what went wrong and an understanding of the height of humanity. We wanted to emerge with the highest civilized values possible, if we were able to survive in the outside world.

In the middle of the clock, we painted the Earth as if it was laid flat, so we could draw lines from the events outside of the clock to the place on earth that they happened. We also prepared a written description for the historical depictions of events. What was clear was that man progressed very slowly at first, when the pace of life and innovation barely changed. Man then used his intellect to improve his dominance on earth. Our theory was that newfound knowledge created new inventions and accelerated change and the pace of life. At a certain point too much knowledge pushed the pace of change too fast overwhelming man who became too chaotic because of the rapid change.

Our debate on pinpointing the exact time in which man's ascent peaked and his descent began was interesting.

Holly said it was the invention of the cellular phone, leading to the handheld device being used all day and night, resulting in rapid new physical changes that our bodies could not handle.

Adam and Grace thought it was the industrial revolution, which led to constant manufacturing improvements until man was unnecessary. They had an interesting second theory that the world had already come full circle with the end of the Roman Empire and start of the middle Ages. They felt that the Renaissance was the second ascent and that the industrial revolution triggered the descent.

Ethan and Faith said it was the first half of the twentieth century, starting with the Armenian Genocide and World War I and ending with World War II, given the mass murdering of Jews and Gypsies, coupled with the first use of atomic weapons in a war that killed 85,000,000 people.

I thought Ethan and Faith were closest to the turning point, but took the turning point back to the height of deep learning in the late nineteenth century. I chose J.J. Thomson's discovery of the first subatomic particle in 1897 as the turning point. Thomson discovered the electron, for which he received the Nobel Prize in 1906. I felt that the greatest minds of the century—Lincoln, Freud, Pasteur, Thomson, Darwin, and Edison—took us to unprecedented knowledge to benefit man, but that knowledge was too much for mankind to handle. Within the next 140 years, we had become too rapidly altered to recognize that knowledge and the technology the knowledge brought were bringing our ruin. After a few weeks of debate, and most probably out of exhaustion by the others, we settled on my opinion.

In our written description, we highlighted the Renaissance as the peak period of mankind's ideals. The Renaissance planted the seeds of the modern world when the arts, education, pursuit of knowledge, travel, and trade accelerated man's knowledge. It led to great discoveries, which continued into the 1800s.

The Renaissance is also the period of time when the seeds of our demise were sown. Throughout the Renaissance, the world shared knowledge and funded the arts and sciences in pursuit of knowledge to benefit everyone. The new understandings and advances in chemistry, thermodynamics, and weaponry were unrivaled in civilized man's history to that point in time. Man was accelerating his understanding of how the world worked. Scientific thought replaced the religious views that believed the Earth was the center of the universe. Man went from earth, water, air, and fire as chemicals to a full table of elements that could be used for good or bad. Man's accelerated understanding and findings led to an industrial revolution, world trade, and advances in medicine, as well as advances in warfare that would eventually lead to the horrible use of chemical weapons to kill millions in the 20th century.

We chose J.J. Thomson's discovery as the turning point because mankind's journey from caves where he painted large animals on the walls to the discovery that the atom was not the smallest particle should have been enough knowledge. Within a short time after Thompson's discovery, Curie discovered radioactivity in 1898, showing that uranium was breaking down and emitting a tremendous amount of energy, which excited scientists. This achievement was extraordinary, leading a great global scientific and technologic pursuit that lasted until the creation of the nuclear weapons that led us back to the cave. Within 50 years of Thomson's discovery, the United States would drop two fission bombs on Japan, marking the arrival of the nuclear age that would permanently ruin the world less than 140 years later. It took 10,000 years to reach mankind's height and 140 years to go back to the starting point.

From 12 o'clock, we used 3 minutes on the clock to describe the centuries to 4000 BC. We depicted European early modern humans (Cro-Magnon man), who were known to have painted on cave walls, and showed how man's knowledge and discoveries changed him slowly from a hunter-gatherer to farmer, builder, animal-raiser, and metal-user.

We used 3 minutes on our clock for each of the next three centuries, highlighting the height of the Egyptian empire and the breathtaking structures they built, ancient Greek culture, showing how writing, art, sport, science, literature, and remarkable ancient structures were built, and the Ming Dynasty, where literature, painting, poetry, and music flourished.

We then used 4 minutes to display the rise and fall of the Roman Empire, depicted Rome, the remarkable size of the empire, and its influence on the modern world including government, legal systems, newspapers, alphabet, aqueducts, and ended with its adopting Christianity as its empire's religion.

We only gave 1 minute to describe the middle ages from 500 to 1500 AD, primarily to cover the period of time, though it is hard to say mankind, particularly in Europe, discernably changed much during this period. We didn't believe that the superstition and primitive lifestyles that marked this period were any kind of growth or development, and marked it as such in our depictions.

We were fair to history and marked bad events during the ascent and good events during the fall. Mankind was always capable of doing horrible things to his fellow man throughout his rise and good during our fall. We painted those points in history where we saw civilized man at his worst, just like we highlighted the positive events and contributions to civilized man that occurred during man's demise. We highlighted man's ability to kill his fellow man, rebellion of masses against control of wealth and power by a small percentage of people, and slavery. Some of the images and events we painted and described were: the mass murder in Carthage by the Romans beginning in 149 BC, where of 400,000 residents (30,000 soldiers), 360,000 were killed and the remainder enslaved, The Yellow Turbin Rebellion by peasants in China that killed 3 to 7 million people from 184–205 AD; the English, Portuguese, French, and Dutch slave traders who profited from the sale of human beings in the Americas, and the Wounded Knee Massacre in 1890, where US soldiers were given medals of honor for massacring Spotted Elk's Miniconjou Lakota Sioux and Hunkpapa Sioux men, women, and children after displacing them (though this is one small example of how Native American Indians were completely abused and eradicated by the European migration to North America).

We gave 10 minutes of the ascent on the clock to highlight the Renaissance, covering 1500-1760. It is important to see the roots of a faster pace of change in man's lifestyle and ability to acquire wealth and power coming from this period of time. The Renaissance was the social, cultural, and knowledge-bridge between the end of the Middle Ages in about 1500 and the beginning of modern man in the early 1800s. Renaissance, or rebirth, was a rekindling of the beauty of ancient Greek and Roman culture. It brought globalization of trade, deep thinking, and an explosion of funding for art and higher learning, where science started taking the place of God. This was the opposite of the superstitious and primitive feel of the prior Middle Ages.

We gave 1760 to 1897 the last 3 minutes of the ascent to 6 o'clock, highlighting the Industrial Revolution when the transition to new machine manufacturing processes and explaining how thermodynamics would become more important. We pointed out on the canvas that Adam and Grace had indicated this was the start of the end because the use of machinery to do what people used to do started here. We also highlighted the French Revolution and its critical battle against a small group of wealthy aristocrats that led to the development of the middle class in France. This was a critical point in world history because 1–2 percent of the people controlled all of the power and wealth (something that repeated itself in America in the early 21rst century when 1-2 percent of the people controlled 8o plus percent of all new money earned). We depicted the Civil War to highlight Lincoln's fight to abolish slavery. We displayed the great inventions of Edison and the work of Freud, Marx, Pasteur, and Darwin. The final picture 6 o'clock was of Thomson's discovery that the atom was not the smallest particle. From this point, every field of study began accelerating its knowledge and understanding. With such immense knowledge, we should have reached new heights. That we reached new lows and destroyed our planet after this discovery, instead of benefitting mankind, was hard to accept.

The first 8 minutes on the left side of the clock covered 1897–1945 and had sections for World War I, the Armenian Genocide, World War II, and the Holocaust and ended with two mushroom clouds for the nuclear warheads dropped on Japan. This period of time represented the absolute worst of man up to this point in world history. Man demonstrated that he was capable of using advancements in knowledge to create nuclear bombs and commit the most horrific acts in history against his fellow man. We showed that 39,000,000 lives were lost in World War I and 50–85 million in World War II, making it the deadliest conflict in the history of the world to that point. It is hard to explain how the great ideals and knowledge generated during the Renaissance resulted in people trying to kill each other rather than understand each other, but that is sadly what happened. We reached our highest points of learning in the late 1800s, but didn't know that future generations would enhance that knowledge to commit horrors rather than good.

With the remaining 22 minutes on the clock, we devoted 9 minutes for 1945–2000, 3 minutes for 2000–2010, 4 minutes for 2010–2020, 5 minutes for 2020–2030, and 1 minute for 2031-2032, which was simply a mushroom cloud marking mankind coming full circle and needing our cave to survive. We depicted the nonviolent movement let by Mahatma Gandhi in India and Martin Luther King Jr. as examples of good in this period of decline.

The period from 1945 to 2000 was clearly a period of time when every passing year led to an increased pace of life. We wanted to show the transition in lifestyle from the early part to the latter part of this period showing how society changed so quickly. The pace of life was slow and wholesome in the 1950s, when the family was depicted in media in a clean, wholesome, and modest manner. Mom cooked dinner and everyone sat down to eat as a family and the kids said sir and ma'am. The 1960s began with that clean '50s family image, but represented a great period of social revolution, like the hippie movement, where the individual was liberated sexually and spiritually. In a way this change was a complete180 degrees turn from the 1950's clean and wholesome feel. Along with widespread use of drugs for the first time, this period countered the ideal family depicted in the 1950s media. Throughout the coming decades, the family became less important, divorce rates went up, and the individual became more important than the group.

Technological improvements in the 1980s delivered the first personal computer and the internet as achievements during a period of great economic growth. The 1990s were a critical period that allowed technology to invade and change the way humans lived and communicated. Alternative lifestyles, body art, extreme sports, and violent video games, all were born and grew in popularity as the individual was celebrated more and more during this period. Technology developed further with the pager and then the cellular phone, which brought tremendous change to the way people lived their lives by creating an immediacy and speed for personal communications. The combination of the internet blossoming, communications changing, the family becoming a less important a structure, technology growing at light-speed, and the importance of the individual created a perfect storm that married self-absorbed individuals with habit-changing technological devices and applications, resulting in a new world full of willing technology lovers and test subjects.

In the section for the 2000s, we depicted and described the horrific rise of terrorism. We displayed the attacks on the World Trade Center in New York and how terrorism expanded rapidly. We described the growth of the internet, the birth of social networks with the arrival of

Facebook, awareness of global warming causing changes to the environment with the warmest decade on record, and the arrival of the smartphone, depicted with the first iPhone in 2007.

We discussed the explosion in cellular phone use throughout the decade, setting the stage for the handheld device to be the newest habit-forming product through which people communicated and developed online personas. The written narrative focused on how rapid technological change was creating rapid changes in lifestyles and habits with new products and social media applications which resulted in people transferring their daily living experience online.

The section with the 2010s was depicted as a period of growing chaos, both individually and globally, among the nations. The images depicted the rapid dwindling of the middle class, which created a small wealthy ruling class controlling 85 percent of all new money earned and who had no interest in allowing other non-rulers to join them. Then, there was the global chaos related to terrorism and a buildup of weaponry, a growing separation between the tech savvy young and older generation that didn't readily adapt to every new technology development, the first serious nuclear threat against the United States (since the 1960s) made by North Korea, and the formation of a dangerous axis of evil against the free world, led by Iran, Russia, and China.

We showed how countries were at odds with each other and that within those countries the individuals were at odds with themselves. We introduced the theory that the global universal language of technology was leading to less understanding and cooperation between the peoples of the world, and within each of the countries, individuals were planting the seeds of revolution by their protests and riots against their fellow citizens. The written description showed how the pace of life and information was coming too fast, leading to growing chaos in the individual.

As an aside, having lived through this period of time and studied history, the developing divide between the wealthy and everyone else from 2010 on contributed to the seeds of revolution, just as they had throughout history. The world was more complex than at any point in its history, but the one historical fact that pretty much always leads to revolution is the domination of the masses and control of almost all wealth by the few. You can pick and choose examples in almost every century from among the French Revolution, The Peasants revolt in England in 1381, The Bolotnikov Rebellion in Russia for the abolition of serfdom in 1606... the wealthy in industrialized countries were in power, were very corrupt, were greedy, had no interest in elevating others, and used the highly expensive legal system to get away with fraud. Additionally, the wealthy committed crimes against the poor and got away with it, even blaming the poor for the crimes they committed.

The wealthy in the 2010's could be defined as a combination of the political class, large corporations, technology giants who were brain-hacking the masses, wealthy businesspeople, and bribed government workers who implemented targeted executions against rivals or opponents of the wealthy. It was a rigged game. The non-wealthy didn't stand a chance. The problem was made even worse as the masses around the world were addicted to and distracted by their smartphones to understand what was happening to them. The slow reaction allowed the wealthy to go unchallenged for most of the decade.

The 2020s were depicted as a horrible period of time. We showed how the period brought out the worst of man. Terrorism was rampant globally as the disenchanted and hopeless were easy recruits. Cyber warfare made the internet more dangerous each year and was the tool of choice for aggressive countries. Revolutions spread through almost every industrialized country as the political process and government institutions failed and the axis of evil with Russia, China, and Iran got set to battle against Europe, the Americas, moderate Arab states, and non-aggressive countries in Asia. The great epidemics were detailed and depicted. The break-up of the EU and the fall of the central government in the United States were also highlighted. Mass population moves, food shortages, armed patrols, and curfews were shown. We detailed the period and described the unraveling of civilized man's foundations, ideals, and institutions.

We put the mushroom cloud spread from 1 minute to 12 to 12 o'clock to signal the end of mankind's rule of the earth.

When we finished, I would often sit alone, looking at this massive canvas that told so much history, and try to understand what we could have done to convince people to observe, study, understand, and act to save mankind and the planet. The guilt at surviving was something I was never really comfortable with. Eight billion people died, wasting the efforts and contributions of billions of prior lives who lived feeling they were building a better world.

Time was something we had plenty of, so I spent hundreds of hours trying to understand the underlying cause of our fall. We had come so far by 1897. Why did we use our height of knowledge for destruction? How did we turn into mass murderers instead of becoming more civilized? I thought for hours and days and years, but I could not come up with a reasonable explanation.

The only theory I ever thought was plausible goes back to the old saying, "ignorance is bliss." Was too much knowledge bad? Did too much information in 1897 drive us insane by leading to the misuse of the knowledge and man's darkest hour with the largest loss of life in human history in 1945, followed by the technological age, further driving us into chaos and destruction? I believe there was something to this theory because it matched the history in our painting. Technology spurred change that was not understood, was misused, and continued to push accelerating changes without ever understanding that our bodies and minds were not meant for this phenomena.

Obviously, a series of complicated global circumstances also contributed to civilized man destroying the world. Greed, terrorism, corruption, abuse of nature, racism, anger, political sabotage, economic negligence, disappearance of the middle class globally, and ego all contributed. Many of these were linked to or had roots in technology. Technology delivered the tools and weapons that abused the natural world nature, technology created the devices that attracted our young, technology created the robots and artificial intelligence that replaced men in high-paying jobs, and technology affected ego. Technology also sent us so much information, much of which was fake information, and we were unable to sift what items required us to act. What do you act on when you are bombarded with disinformation? We inhabit a body meant to process one thing at a time. When it becomes two items, then four items, then 20 items at a time, how can anyone know which is the most important to action when another 20 bits are coming on top of that? Too much information drove the individual and the whole world insane.

The painting helped us understand what went wrong. We then set about our next major task, which was to figure out what our ideals and vision for the future should be. The debate was lively and often disrupted by the little ones running around. The deep thinking on this came from Holly and me, who set about creating a platform for our future existence.

With a blank canvas to start with, we wanted to correct the greatest mistakes made by civilized man. Upon discussion with Holly, who felt the longest fight in mankind's history was women's fight for equality, we came up with our vision for mankind's future.

1.　　Women and men are to be treated as equals.

2.　　The family and group are more important than any individual.

3.   We must respect the natural integrity of the Earth, which nurtures us, at all times.

4.   No technology besides for the common good.

5.   Knowledge is to be used only for the common good.

6.   No individual is more important than another individual, with the following exception: opinions of the elders carry more weight than opinions of the younger ones.

7.   All jobs are to be rotated among each member of our family unless someone is physically unable to perform the job.

8.   Each individual above 10 would vote on any issue that affected the group or in a dispute, with a 85 percent majority needed for approving any serious topic brought up to a vote.

9.   Marriage is a serious, lifelong commitment never to be broken.

10.   We strive to build each other up and help one another, not tear each other down and not help each other.

Everything we did as a group relayed back to these ideals for guidance. It ran our political, legal, labor, farming, educational, and social processes. These rules encouraged knowledge for good and promoted building our fellow man up rather than tearing him down.

The following years were uneventful accept for the arrival of the new generations, the first in man's history to be born and not see the outside world.

Chapter 12

2068

Our knowledge of the outside world since 2032 was limited to the information we could gather from the periscope. This job was the only one that was not rotated. Since Grace and Faith had been in charge for so long, we felt they had the best perspective to notice changes in the colors and textures. They created the following series of consolidated notes, broken into 6-year periods, which showed the following:

2032–2037

The world looks gray, cold, and devoid of wildlife. Dirty snow is on the ground year-round. It doesn't snow or rain much, but looks like it is cold most of the year.

2037–2043

No signs of life. There seems to be some warming during the summer months, though not all the snow melts. Gray is the predominant color. There is much less snow and rain than before 2031. There are infrequent signs of bluer skies in the summer months.

2043–2049

The world is becoming less gray and more bluish in color. The snow melts in the summer but the trees still look dead. No wildlife has been seen. There are signs of increased rain and snowfall, but still less than the norms before 2032. Summers are getting longer and new trees are sprouting among the older, dead trees. There is more sunlight every year, but things look cold and icy.

2049–2055

New trees are now growing high and have smaller than usual leaf growth. The amounts of rain and snowfall have stayed the same for about 10 years . The gray is gone, but it has not been replaced by brilliant whites and blues in the sky. There is no animal life. The snow is melting earlier in the spring and summer and is gone by June.

2055–2061

We think we are reaching a turning point for the Earth. Things are almost normal in terms of weather. The trees that sprouted in the 2040s mostly died or stayed small. They are being replaced by trees that are growing at a faster rate and bigger size. Rain is increasing, as is snowfall.

2061–2068

Every year becomes more normal based on our memories before coming into the cave. It appears as though the outside world has gone through repairing itself and preparing for the next inhabitants who will live there. The blues in summer are almost normal and are becoming more brilliant. There was a massive amount of rain in the fall of 2067, followed by a heavy snowfall throughout the winter of 2067–2068. The new trees are thriving, the dead trees have disappeared, and the world looks like it has recovered.

In April 2068, we were all shocked when Faith screamed when the periscope seemed to have a mind of its own and was being pushed up and down. Grace was hit in the head by one of the handlebars as she was trying to gain control. When she finally got control, the screen was dark. She could not make out what it was. After a few seconds, when the perpetrator backed off a bit, Grace saw that it was a bear, the first sign of life anyone had seen in over 35 years.

The finding was significant to us. The world appeared to be regenerating to the point life could exist on the surface. That meant food was available, the radiation levels were likely low or gone, and we were approaching the end of our days in the cave.

I can't say that I was as excited as a kid in a candy store, but I was pretty happy to hear about that bear, as dangerous as he might be. The Earth had recovered and we could prepare for exiting the cave safely.

We decided to wait a few more months before exiting, which was four years earlier than planned. Though we had enough food to survive longer, we felt that seeing natural life meant that the worst was over and we could soon leave safely.

We had grown to a family of 31. We had grown so large I don't even remember everyone's name. While all that growth would normally be cause for chaos, the rules we set for living our lives, the lack of technology in our environment, and the focus on the whole quieted any natural chaos created by the young children. It was a matter of teaching children that they needed to care about everyone else as much as they cared about themselves. We lived a calm, happy life with excellent communication. Of course the kids got wild and needed to be taught what our expectations were, but by ten years of age, each new child adapted fully to the group's importance as a whole.

Holly and I stressed to Adam, Grace, Ethan, and Faith how important it was for them to make sure they adhered to our family's vision and be prepared for anything once we emerged. We knew very little except that there was a bear that came from somewhere. At the very least, that bear would be faced, but at the very most, no one could know. Ethan didn't think anyone could have survived another month, yet alone many years out there, but he wasn't sure. We discussed that we should be ready for anything.

We prepared our exit plan. Adam and his oldest son, Jimmy, would go down the underground river and then make their way back up to the tunnel leading to the cave. The older kids would start digging out the dirt that the sealed us into the cave and put the dirt in bags (I was holding my promise to keep the cave as close to how I found it as possible). Adam and Jimmy would remove the booby traps I set and dig from the other side after they exited the cave. We would then secure the property, inhabit the house, restore the cave, and convert the warehouse to living space. Then, we would evaluate food resources, evaluate the surrounding areas, and make sure we were safe from any threat.

I started to feel old and felt my body slowing down through the last five years leading to 2068. I felt my time was soon coming to an end and reflected obsessively over Andrea, her loss and how without her, we would have all been dead. The sadness over Andrea and guilt over Ethan was eating at me. So was the guilt over surviving when all others died horrific deaths. The fear and anticipation of repopulating the world after man killed the Earth and all humans kept me feeling very unsettled.

Holly felt my angst the most, as I was very quiet and introverted, and sometimes not focused on what she was saying. Holly was resilient and tough-minded and knew how to survive and do what needed to be done. She knew that she could never replace Andrea and didn't try. She stayed focused on the job at all times in the cave when a less strong person would have crumbled. We were both aging, but Holly was definitely going stronger than I was.

I took solace in the leadership of the kids and the beauty of how they understood our painful history, their importance to man's history, and how important it was for them not to repeat the mistakes made the first time around. Our children, grandchildren, and great-grandchildren were determined to follow our vision and do a better job with this second chance.

Knowing your time is coming is tough. You know it is inevitable; you know it will hurt your loved ones. You feel like there is so much more to do, so much you wanted to do, so much you did wrong, and it is hard to see the positive. I tried the opposite approach to make it through

114

these years. I said to myself, you held your promise to Andrea, assured the family would survive, grew a large family, assured that mankind will have a second chance if in fact we were the last humans alive, raised good boys, and beat self-doubt about going the distance. I also knew that it was not me alone that did this. Andrea was there with me the whole time, giving me strength. I knew exactly what I was going to scream if I made out of the cave: Andrea, my love, you saved us!

Chapter 13 and 1

The Wheel

No one could have thought of all the spare items we would need to survive for decades in a cave. We either invented a solution or we lived without the item. Now it is with the wheel I'm chiseling out of stone so we can try to continue using our wheelbarrow. As I worked on the wheel earlier, I couldn't help but think about the rise and fall of mankind, whose first invention the modern world recognized was the wheel. I'm overwhelmed by the symbolism of the wheel, invented by cavemen on their way to becoming modern man, and of the full circle civilized man had taken. We started by needing caves to protect us from the large predators, only to return to the cave, needing it to protect us from the splitting of the smallest particle known to man, the atom. For all we know, we are the last civilized humans left on Earth.

Our reports from Grace and Faith say that we are close to being able to emerge from the cave. It is now July 4, 2068, and we have spent almost 36 years in our cave. Knowing my life is approaching the end of its cycle, and not knowing if I will see the outside world again, only adds to me feeling overwhelmed. The conflict between exhilaration of surviving and guilt of surviving is one that is impossible to describe because no one on Earth ever had to face what we faced by being lone survivors of a global nuclear war.

Over centuries of mankind's history, to about the year 1900, man had emerged from caves, progressed from being a hunter-gatherer to being modern men and women dominating the planet and attaining unparalleled heights of knowledge, only to allow ourselves to use that knowledge to destroy ourselves in the next 140 years. Man used technology for corrupt purposes and began accepting technology immediately, without knowing that the side effects would eventually lead to natural and individual chaos. Man wasn't meant to live any part of his life anywhere but here on Earth. By the 21st century, technology had created a generation of addicted humans living some or most of their lives in an online fantasy world that distorted and changed the way they lived in the real world. People barely lifted their faces from their smartphones to notice that chaos had gripped the world and was leading to the most destructive, horrific end anyone could have imagined.

While we were certainly more civilized and sophisticated than the first cavemen, we were as certainly in the same condition as our predecessors many centuries earlier. We were probably worse off knowing that all the accumulated knowledge we'd gained and heights we'd scaled instead led to corruption of the technology that killed people, abused the Earth, and create mass chaos globally. Too much knowledge/technology was our tower of babel leading to global chaos.

I reflect on how 50 years earlier, in 2018, Andrea came up with the plan to find a cave suitable for long-term survival, given the warning signs we saw in the world around us. As I think and write about my dearest Andrea and look at her urn that holds her ashes, my mind races through the past. Flashes of what happened to Ethan, Faith's growth, Holly, the expansion of the family, the combined feeling of exhilaration and depression of surviving the events is overwhelming. I find myself crying like a baby. I don't understand why I'm so emotional tonight after 36 years, but for some reason, tonight feels different.

***

The above words were the last my father would write in his journal documenting his remarkable story of survival and role as caretaker of humanity. My father, Noah, had a stroke later that night. He lived almost three years longer, though it was hard for him to speak and walk. He couldn't write anymore and asked that we keep this journal as a link between our first and second tries at getting inhabiting the earth right.

My parents saw the future before others and saved all of us from a horrific end. My dad was ridiculed by many, fought his own doubts, protected all of us from a horrible end, and will be known as humanity's caretaker. He taught us what was best about mankind and what our ideals should be. Though haunted by the pain of losing my mom and what happened to my brother Ethan, my Dad endured and finished his goal of protecting us until we could safely emerge from the cave that protected and nurtured us. He never lost focus, despite the heavy burdens placed on him.

My dad lived to emerge from the cave with us. Upon exiting, we spread my mother's ashes over the newly reborn land. Even after having losing most of his ability to speak, we all heard my dad whisper, as we spread our mother's ashes, "Andrea, my love, you saved us!"